GROWN-UP CHRISTMAS LIST

GROWN-UP CHRISTMAS LIST

OCEAN CITY BOARDWALK SERIES
BOOK 5

DONNA FASANO

Find the author:

Facebook – Facebook.com/DonnaFasanoAuthor

Twitter – Twitter.com/DonnaFaz

Pinterest – Pinterest.com/DonnaFaz

Instagram – Instagram.com/Donna_Fasano

Contents

Dedication

This story is dedicated to reader Leann Griffiths, who entered the *Favorite Christmas Song Contest* and, in winning, ended up choosing the title of this book. Grown Up Christmas List happens to be one of my favorite holiday songs. Thank you for entering the contest, Leann, and for choosing such a fabulous song. I hope you enjoy the book. I am both humbled by and eternally grateful for enthusiastic readers like you.

Introduction

Dina Griffin flees a dangerous situation and ends up in Ocean City, Maryland where she hopes to spend the holidays in hiding. Trusting no one, she wants only one thing this Christmas—to feel safe. Then Officer Gav Thomas threatens to arrest her for shoplifting. *Shoplifting?*

Gav is certain there's something Dina isn't telling him about her visit to his seaside town, so he devises a means to stick close to the vulnerable beauty. An unexpected attraction sparks, fierce enough to heat up the salt-tinged, wintry nights.

But the trouble Dina had hoped to escape arrives at her doorstep, bringing with it stark-raving fear and the realization that she *must* place her trust in someone.

Is Gav really just a local cop... or is he Dina's guardian angel?

CHAPTER ONE

Lively strains of Christmas music floated from somewhere in the rafters as Dina Griffin let her gaze rove over the rows of shampoo bottles lining the shelf. Lemon yellow, bright purple, jarring chartreuse, the plastic containers came in a rainbow of colors, each competing to catch the eye of shoppers. There were products that guaranteed help for damaged split ends; others promising shine and curl; and still others offering to clarify, volumize, or medicate. The abundance of choices astonished her. And to think, all she'd ever expected from her shampoo was clean hair. It wasn't as if she'd never been shopping, but her busy life usually had her running in, snapping up her tried-and-true bargain brand, and going on her way. Studying the bottles closer, she read phrases like *moisture milk*, *herbal escapes*, *essential oils*, *vitamin-laced*, and *tea therapy*.

Tea therapy?

A few steps further brought her to the matching conditioners, also in a mind-boggling, kaleidoscopic variety. Then came the specialty shampoos for dandruff and hair loss and itchy, scaly scalp conditions. And nits.

Lice. Ew.

Dina shivered inside her bulky winter coat as she ambled along, feigning great interest in the items on display.

She reached the end of the aisle, and just as she stepped out to make her way around the shelving unit, the electronic doors at the front of the store slid open, drawing her attention.

A cop entered the pharmacy, and adrenalin shot through Dina like a high voltage jolt. Perspiration broke out on the back of her neck and her heart began to thud. She turned her head away, dipping both her chin and her gaze as she sunk back as far as possible into her wide-brimmed hood.

Mustering a calm nonchalance she certainly did not feel, she skirted the tall, end cap display of hard pretzels and slipped into the neighboring aisle. She stopped halfway down and perused the first-aid section with enough focus to lead anyone who might notice her to think her life depended on finding the perfect band-aid.

The officer wasn't here for her. He wasn't. He couldn't possibly know she'd run from the police in Baltimore. He couldn't.

Dina dared not chance looking behind her, but her stomach sank when she sensed someone approaching. As the person got closer, she could feel the mass of him. It was the cop. Had to be. And the man must be built as solid as a brick wall.

He wasn't here for her. He wasn't. She repeated the silent mantra, bending at the waist and grasping the first package within reach. Tweezers, she realized. Silver. Pointy-tipped.

Her fingers were trembling, so she released the plastic and cardboard container. However, when she pulled her hand back, her coat sleeve caught the edge of several packages and tweezers went tumbling like inept circus acrobats. Dina scrambled, snatching them up, and hurrying to re-hang them on the metal display hook.

The cop stopped directly behind her. She straightened, closed her eyes, and drew in a breath in an effort to calm her anxiety. And that's when she smelled him.

The scent of fresh cut sandalwood tickled her nose. Warm and slightly spicy.

He cleared his throat and her eyes flew open.

Could he have picked up a splinter on the job somehow? Be in dire need of a pair of pointy-tipped tweezers? Maybe he'd cut himself shaving and needed one of those small circular band-aids. That would be her luck, all right. A splinter-laden, razor-nicked cop in need of first-aid supplies, and she just happened to be standing right in front of the display.

Her only goal in walking around the pharmacy had been to warm up a little. Although the day was sunny and the outside temperatures on the mild side this morning, it was still winter, and the damp concrete she'd slept on had left her chilled to the bone. Her hips had been aching and her feet had felt like brittle bricks of ice when she'd arrived, and she'd just wanted to limber up, work the cold out of her joints and toes in a heated environment.

"Miss? I need you to come with me."

How could he possibly have known...

Dina hesitated, nerves forcing her to swallow even though her mouth had gone as dry as coarse sand. She was *not* going back to Baltimore. Not until she absolutely had to. What compelled her next action, she had no idea—fear, panic, sheer survival instinct—but she spun on her heel and glared into his face.

"I'm not going anywhere with you. This is a free country, and I've got rights. I'm staying right here, and there's not a damn thing you can do about it."

An instant of shock registered on his face. But his jaw quickly set, his lips flattened, and he seemed to grow three inches when he squared his shoulders and straightened his spine.

Oh, Lord, save her. Had she really just gone all rebel on an officer of the law?

"Yeah," he said, his tone soft but firm, "this *is* a free country. And you do have rights. Just so long as you don't take things that don't belong to you." He pinched the sleeve of her coat between his fingers. "So put back whatever it is you've stolen, and come up to the front counter with me. We need to have a chat with the manager."

"Wait. What are you talking about?"

He muttered under his breath, then said loud enough for her to hear, "Being uncooperative is only going to make matters worse for you. Your parents are already going to be upset when I call them. It's bad enough you're cutting school. Shoplifting is a serious offence."

Cutting... What? *Shoplifting?* She looked at him as if he'd suddenly sprouted a grotesque, green beard.

"All right." He sighed. "We can play this any way you want."

Her bravado withered like a sycamore leaf in the dead of winter when she felt herself being propelled toward the front of the store. There must have been only an inch of her coat fabric in his grip, but it was enough to force her to toddle along beside his long-legged stride like a twelve-year-old.

Her whole body went hot with utter humiliation.

The store manager, Dina presumed, was the pretty blonde who stood behind the cash register. She had a fresh-faced, just-out-of-high-school look about her, the big wad of gum she nervously chomped on further evidence of her youth.

"So what'd she take?" the girl demanded. "I knew she was up to something."

The officer's attention remained riveted to Dina. "I'm going to have to ask you to empty your pockets."

Dina could no more have stopped her gasp than she could have forced the sea breeze to cease.

"No. I won't." She hated the pleading she heard in her tone as she added, "I haven't taken anything."

A flicker of something softened the cop's brown eyes, but only for an instant before he shook his head and pointed to the counter. "Let's have it. On the counter. Now. Coat pockets. Jean's pockets. Backpack. Everything."

She wasn't normally someone given to bouts of crying or who yielded to doubts or apprehension. But she was tired and achy and filled with the residual fear of having fled a dangerous situation just two short days ago. A lump of raw emotion swelled in her throat and hot tears scorched her eyes sockets.

She would not cry, damn it.

When she spoke, the words grated like a rusty bolt. "I'll do what you ask, but it's under protest. I did not take anything from this store."

The bar of soap in the large, clear plastic bag she tugged from her coat pocket *thunked* against the counter when she dropped it. Ticket stubs for the bus ride that had brought her to town. Several wadded tissues.

"There," the blonde said, satisfaction palpable in the jab of her finger when she pointed, "soap, a toothbrush, a tube of toothpaste. She's been in here two mornings in a row. I knew she was stealing from us, Officer Thomas." Smugly, she added, "I knew it."

Dina lifted her chin and narrowed her eyes at the young woman. "I didn't steal that. I paid for the toothbrush and toothpaste. The soap, too. Yesterday morning." She searched the pockets of her jeans and then slapped a receipt on the counter.

The cop picked up the slip of paper and took a moment to study it. He handed it to the manager. His tone became much less harsh when he asked Dina, "Nothing else in your pockets?"

She'd already set her wallet beside the plastic

bag. She watched him rummage quickly through her backpack.

"Janey," the cop said to the store manager, "there's no fingernail polish in here. You told me you saw her take a bottle of red nail polish."

The blonde looked contrite. "I think what I said was that she *possibly* could have taken—"

"No. You didn't. You were adamant that she took the polish."

Janey's cute face squinched as she whined, "Officer Thomas, Dad docked my pay last week because of shoplifters. He said I wasn't being vigilant enough."

"You cannot go around accusing people of stealing, Janey."

"But I was certain a bottle of polish had gone missing. She's been roaming around, buying nothing, for a solid forty minutes. I'm here by myself. Dad doesn't get in until nine. I didn't know what else to do."

Her only thought to escape this fracas and any further chance that she'd have to interact with the officer, Dina snatched up her things and stuffed them into her backpack. She slung the strap over her shoulder and headed for the front door. She could still hear the two of them going back and forth when bright sunshine hit her face and the cold, salt-tinged breeze snaked its way into her hood and down the neck of her coat. The cooling sensation was actually a relief after that sweat-inducing accusation she'd just endured.

She'd taken several steps across the parking lot when the officer shouted at her from the pharmacy's entrance. Dina wanted to ignore him, wanted to scuttle away and hide like a crab fleeing a hungry seagull, but that behavior would look nothing but suspicious.

Her steps slowed as her nearly non-existent options twirled in her head along with the possible repercussions.

Hearing him jogging toward her, she stopped, let her eyes roll closed, and murmured softly to herself, "Please, don't let me say anything that gets me into any more trouble. I just want a little peace. *Please*."

Dina had no idea to whom she whispered the words. Her mother would automatically offer an approving nod at what she'd call a "prayer to the angels." Dina wasn't so sure about all the angelic mysteries she'd been spoon-fed while growing up.

Not that she deemed it total baloney; no, she preferred to keep an open mind about such esoteric things. Just because a belief lacked tangible evidence was no reason to disregard it. And as her mom always said, nonbelievers had no solid proof, either.

What Dina *could* say was that her whispered mantras habitually sprang to her lips at times of great stress. If nothing else, the words encouraged her to be more mindful of her behavior, of her words, and of her thoughts. All perfectly good practices as far as she was concerned.

Just as the officer touched her on the shoulder, she opened her eyes, forced a smile on her mouth, and turned to face him.

"Hey, listen," he said, "I'm awfully sorry about what happened in there."

"No problem." Dina did her best to keep her attitude friendly. Light and breezy. "Really. I'm fine. Everything is all good."

"Janey's young. Over protected by helicopter-parents."

The bright, morning sunlight made him squint and burnished his brown hair with deep chestnut highlights. Noticing attractive men was not on

Dina's To-Do list while she was in Ocean City. Her plan included two actions only: keeping her head low and remaining inconspicuous for the next couple of weeks.

"I understand," she told him. "Like I said, I am one hundred percent fine. No worse for the wear at all."

His jaw squared and he shifted his weight on his feet. "I let her know she owed you an apology."

"That's not necess—"

"And I also made it perfectly clear," he continued, "that she was not to call the police unless she or one of her employees actually witnessed a crime being committed."

"It would be good if that didn't happen to anyone else. Being called a thief is about as fun as participating in the Polar Plunge."

"I can imagine. Come on back inside." He made a small waving motion with his hand. "Give Janey a chance to tell you how sorry she is. And then you can finish up your shopping."

Dina wasn't going back in that pharmacy. No way. No how. It didn't matter if the zombie apocalypse had the undead shuffling across the parking lot toward her.

"I'm good," she said, nodding in emphasis. "I don't need to go back in. I got what I was after."

He stared for a moment, digesting what she'd said. His smile slipped, and then the tiniest of frowns marred the space between his eyebrows.

Her lips parted and she inhaled sharply.

"*Heat*," she hurried to explain. "I went inside to warm up. I was freezing."

"Ah, so that explains the hood."

Without thinking, she reached up and fingered the edge of the wool fabric. "Well, hoods *were* invented to protect the head from cold temperatures."

"True," he said, "but people don't normally shop with them pulled up over their faces. I've got to tell you, you had a bit of a gangsta' look going on there."

"That's not against the law, is it?"

Crap. Stop poking the bear, Dina. Had she been alone, she'd have voiced the thought out loud. Then again, had she been alone she wouldn't have had cause to do any verbal sparring.

He burst out laughing. "Give the lady a prize. She's right a second time."

The sound of his laughter took her off guard

and she felt momentarily breathless. Standing this close to him, she couldn't help but notice the rich, warm gold that flecked his brown eyes, and his smile was downright infectious. Merely for something to do with her hands, she tossed back the hood of her coat, and immediately, the breeze blew a strand of her hair across her face.

His grin went lopsided. "I was only teasing you about the gangster look. Honest."

Humor budded to life inside her, but the riot of nervous energy simmering in her chest prevented her from doing anything but stare. She *wanted* to laugh with him; she just couldn't.

That uniform he wore sparked a sense of dread in her, and that seemed fairly normal, given her predicament. So why did this bantering feel so darned delicious?

"Aw, you're still upset." He tilted his head. "I can tell."

Finally, she tilted her head. "You threatened to call my parents."

He looked like a cute puppy who'd gotten caught chewing an expensive shoe.

"Sorry," he murmured. "With that hood pulled

up, I thought you were a teen. I can see now you're much older."

"Well, thank you very much."

"Wait. That's not what I meant. Not at all." The sound he emitted was a cross between a chuckle and a groan. "I should shut up. I'm only making things worse." Then his gaze lit and his brows arched. "Why don't you let me take you to breakfast? You know, to make up for this whole mess."

"Oh, no." She lifted her hand, palm out, and shook her head. Then she instantly checked her tone. She added, "Thank you, but that isn't necessary."

Once again, his smile waned, but now he looked solemn.

"I know it's not necessary."

Since following her outside, he'd changed. His voice had lost every nuance of its professional, hard edges, the ones that had induced that heavy feeling of being trapped when he'd forced her to empty her pockets. In fact, it had gone all warm and inviting.

"The truth of the matter is," he continued, "I'm obviously to blame for some of that mix up in there. Besides assuming you were just a kid intent on getting away with something, I should have asked Janey more questions before I approached you." His head bobbed a little. "I should have waited. Watched. I should have shown more patience."

She didn't care how dreamy his eyes were or how infectious his smile, spending any more time with this man than was absolutely necessary was not only a bad idea, it could be extremely risky.

"You were only doing your job." She hitched her backpack higher onto her shoulder. "I appreciate your offer, but—"

"I feel bad.... Uh, I don't even know your name." He blinked. "I don't want this to give you a bad impression of our town." He reached up and scrubbed at his jaw. "We accused you of shoplifting. Janey was irresponsible. I was heavy-handed. Not to mention presumptuous. And wrong." He shook his head woefully. "This is just a very bad start to everyone's day, now, isn't it?"

Dina took in his wrinkled brow, his contrite expression. The man looked positively wretched.

Then his tone brightened as he added, "Lucky for both of us, we can always begin again, right?

So what do you say? Let's start over. It's time for my break. And I'm starved. We can walk across Coastal Highway to one of my favorite places to eat. The sound of the waves. The sparkle of the sunlight on the ocean. A hot cup of coffee will warm you right up. And a stack of fluffy, buttery blueberry pancakes will set everything right. I just know it."

If the smile he'd offered before had been alluring, this one was enough to melt a woman's heart to the point that it oozed down her ribcage to pool in a sappy mess in the pit of her belly.

That she was even considering his offer was crazy. Utterly nut-house insane.

But what happened in the pharmacy *had* been a mistake. She'd compounded her own fear by thinking he knew she was on the run. He hadn't known. No one in Baltimore knew *where* she was, and no one in Ocean City knew *who* she was. Now that she'd had time to calmly realize that, there was no reason for her to believe that her secret was anything but safe.

The man had offered to buy her a meal. Hadn't she slept on a cement slab last night in an effort to conserve her cash? This was, as her mother would have claimed, an unexpected blessing from the Universe. To refuse to accept could very well be an insult.

Oh, man. A silent moan reverberated through her mind. Her angel-worshiping mother would be so proud of her. *Gah!*

There was no need to make up fancy notions or fearful justifications. If she wanted to accept the pancakes the guy was offering, she should just do it. He was nice enough, now that he wasn't trying to arrest her. He was a good looking man. But, of course, that was just a fortunate fluke, right? The most important thing was that her secret was safe. And there was no reason why it wouldn't remain that way.

Dina sighed, the pent-up tension in her body gradually dissipating. She offered him an open and easy smile and said, "Maybe we *should* start over."

His blatant pleasure made her insides go weak.

"I'm Gav," he told her, reaching out his hand. "Gav Thomas."

Her fingers slid against his until their palms connected in a snug grasp. Gav gave her hand a firm shake.

"Dina," she told him. "Call me Dina."

CHAPTER TWO

The pancakes were light and buttery, the strips of bacon delectably smoky and fried crisp. Dina took a bite of pancake and savored the flavor of the warm, plump blueberry that burst between her molars.

"Mmmm." Sweet maple syrup made her lips sticky, and as soon as she swallowed, she licked them, and then wiped her mouth with a paper napkin. "These are *so* good."

He nodded behind his coffee mug. "There's nothing a stack of pancakes can't fix."

The restaurant he'd brought her to, The Sunshine Café, was located right on the boardwalk. Dina couldn't help glancing out the front window at the ocean in the distance, the muffled sound of waves washing against the shore in exotic harmony.

Two elderly gentleman sat at the counter, discussing local politics, and the owner, Gav had introduced the woman as Cathy, stood at the grill back in the kitchen which was visible from the dining area. But despite the homey atmosphere emanating from the tidy café, Dina remained on her guard.

Several times, Gav had asked her questions. His casual tone had made the queries seem innocent enough, but there was an unmistakable probing undercurrent to them. Each time, she'd been able to deflect and evade. She didn't want to tell him a bunch of personal information, but neither did she want to out and out lie to the man.

Sensing he was about to make more inquiries, she beat him to the punch with a question of her own.

"So have you always wanted to be a cop?"

He nodded. "I have. My dad's a police officer, and both his brothers are, too."

"Wow, that's a pretty strong family influence."

"Maybe," he told her. "I had a good childhood. Strict, by some people's estimation probably. A lot of people complain about their parents. I'm happy to say I don't have much to complain about. Their focus was on doing the right thing. Helping others. Doing your best at whatever you set out to do."

Dina grinned. "I'll bet you were a Boy Scout."

"Damn straight." He chuckled, and then pride tinged his voice as he added, "Eagle Scout."

"Whoa." Although she meant to tease him, she really was impressed. She cut another triangle of pancake, speared it with her fork and dragged it through the pool of butter-laden syrup on her plate. "You're from around here? Your dad and uncles work for Ocean City?"

"No. I grew up in Western Maryland. Dad worked for the Cumberland Police Department. One uncle took a job in Philadelphia. The other in Baltimore."

Her gut clenched, but she continued to slowly chew.

"When you want to work in law enforcement," he continued, "you usually have to go wherever the job openings are."

She took a sip of orange juice, and then said, "So

you came to Ocean City because that's where the job was?"

He held her gaze for a moment, his brown eyes contemplative.

"Well," he said, drawing out the word like a song note, "not really. I had to work hard to land this position. I visited Ocean City with friends as a teen. I loved summers at the beach."

Dina blurted, "Me, too!"

As soon as the words left her mouth, she checked herself.

"Ocean City holds a lot of good memories for me," he said. "I decided I'd like to live and work here. But it's taken a lot of time."

"Oh?"

"I graduated from the Academy eight years ago." He set down his mug. "I worked as a seasonal officer for the town every summer since I completed my training. I applied for every full-time, year-round position posted by the town as did hundreds of other people. Back in September, I finally landed a job."

Dina set her fork down. If she ate another bite, she'd explode. "You came back for eight summers before getting a full-time job? You weren't kidding when you said you worked hard. That's dedication. Congratulations."

"Thanks."

She picked up her napkin and wiped her fingertips. "So are you loving it?"

"I am. The winters, I'm learning, are pretty quiet. Which is nice."

Dina muttered, "Save for the shoplifter here and there."

He grinned. "Yeah." Then he arched his brows. "Winters might be quiet, but the toy drives are killer."

"Toy drives?"

Gav nodded. "Tradition dictates that the new guy organizes the holiday toy drive."

She frowned. "But Christmas is just around the corner. Shouldn't the toys be gathered up and delivered by now? The parents of those kids will need time to wrap the presents."

One corner of his mouth pulled back in a grimace and misery overtook his expression as he nodded. "Yeah, ninety-nine percent of my co-workers have finished up their lists, and gathered their toys. You're right. I should be finished, too, but I've run into a little trouble." His chin lifted. "You sound like you have some experience at this."

"Um, yeah," she admitted, feeling there was no way not to. "Helping the needy. It's important. I've volunteered with charity programs. Ah, food drives, toy drives, clothing. Um, up in... you know, back home."

Dina heard her choppy, awkward phrasing, but could do nothing to prevent it. She never realized the ease with which she normally talked about herself, her activities, her thoughts, her home town. Guarding her personal information took concentration.

"I've had a lot of businesses and private residents promise toys," he explained, "but only about half have actually followed through."

"Gosh, that's terrible." Dina reached for her glass and swirled the tiny bit of orange pulp left in the bottom.

"I'll get it done."

The doubt she saw reflected in his eyes belied the bravado in his tone.

He shifted on the seat, caught the proprietor's eye and pointed to his coffee cup in a silent appeal for a refill. When he leveled his gaze on Dina again, hope had chased away the shadows.

"Hey, you wouldn't have the time to help me, would you? You know, ride around in the evening, pick up toys from the elderly people who don't drive? Stop in at the businesses and give 'em a little prod?" His mouth screwed up. "I think my biggest problem is that I don't like to make people feel guilty. You know, the donors, I mean."

"Make them feel guilty?" She chuckled. "Oh, Gav, I have no doubt I could help you. You're looking at this all wrong."

He arched his brows in interest.

"Many businesses only donate a fraction of what they're able to." Dina leaned toward him. "I've heard that from more than one business owner." She shifted on the bench seat. "Think about this from the angle of the kids. Talk about the kids. Give people a few details. Not names or anything like that, of course. But *needs*. Name the needs, and people will come through for you. That's been my experience, anyway."

"Sounds like you're just what I need. I can't go tonight. I've got a meeting at the precinct. But tomorrow evening? We do a little collecting and then grab a bite to eat. What do you think?"

Ignoring the squeamish feeling in her gut, she paused for a moment and then forced herself to ask, "This gig doesn't come with any pay, does it?"

The owner of the café arrived at the table with a pot of hot coffee and Gav slid his cup toward her. "Thanks, Cathy," he murmured as the woman filled his mug and then turned to walk away.

To Dina he said, "I don't have a spending account. Sorry. You need a job?"

"I'd feel better if I was making some money while I was in town, yeah," she told him. "Just for the next couple of weeks. Nothing huge. Just a few bucks to get me through the holidays."

"You have experience waiting tables?" Without waiting for an answer, he turned and called out, "Cathy, could you use a waitress?"

The woman turned back to them, one hip jutting. "No. Sorry." She looked at Dina. "But I *could* use a dishwasher. I'm open seven in the morning until three in the afternoon. Breakfast and lunch. Monday's off. Closed Christmas Day. We open at ten on New Year's Day. Minimum wage. I'll split each day's tips with you."

"Wow." Dina couldn't believe her ears. "It would only be temporary."

Cathy nodded. "How soon can you start?"

"I'm available right now," Dina told her. "If that works for you."

"That's great," she said. "Finish your breakfast and your visit. Then clean that table off and we can get acquainted in the kitchen."

"Thanks," Dina told her. "Thank you so much."

The woman smiled, then went back behind the bar to fill the cups of the two men sitting at the counter.

"Wow," Dina repeated, continued awe in her voice. "That was so nice of you. And her. Neither one of you even know me—"

"Hold up," he said, stirring a dollop of cream in his coffee, "you might not thank me when all is said and done. Cathy's a good person, but she doesn't pull any punches. If you don't live up to her expectations, you'll be out the door in a heartbeat."

"I'm not worried," Dina said. "I'll make it work."

"So how long *will* you be in town?" he asked. "You said through the holidays."

"Just until after the first of the year." She stacked

her dishes in a neat pile. "I have to be back for—" She stopped. "Some meetings."

She was getting better. The hesitation this time had been barely perceptible.

"You're spending the holidays with family?" He lifted the mug to his lips.

"I've never spent Christmas at the beach." She smiled, hoping he wouldn't notice her evasive measure. "Thought I'd head down here to see if Ocean City is as nice in the winter as it is in the summer."

Gav chuckled. "It's more serene, I'll say that much. You never said where you're staying."

She hated to lie. It went against every good and moral fiber of her being. She was going to find a hotel room. And soon. But she hadn't found one yet.

Telling him where she'd spent last night was out of the question, so she thought about the hotel she had her eye on.

"It's called Princess something," she said. "The Bay Princess."

"On 81st Street? That's not a hotel, that's a building of condominium units. Are you renting a place there?"

"No. No. I must have gotten the name wrong." She frowned. "I could have sworn the hotel had Bay and Princess in the name."

"Princess Bayside?"

"That's it." Her mouth had gone dusty dry. That was the hotel she saw across the street this morning when she slipped out of the parking garage. "Yeah, I'm sure that's it."

She tossed the balled up napkins on top of the stack of plates, and then she scooted toward the edge of the bench seat. "Listen, I really appreciate your buying me breakfast, Gav. And the help with the job and all. And I meant what I said about your toy drive. I'm happy to help." She stood up and busied herself gathering up utensils. "But I really should get back there and get started. I'd like to make a good impression."

Sliding the dirty dishes onto her forearm, she said, "I'm sure I'll see you around, okay?"

Dina shot him a smile and headed toward the kitchen.

CHAPTER THREE

Under normal circumstances, Gav limited his visits to Cathy's café to once a week. Otherwise, those fluffy pancakes slathered in butter and syrup had the potential to turn into love handles. However, he was headed there now, not for breakfast or even a cup of joe, but because he wanted to check on Dina.

Something wasn't right there. He sensed it in his gut just as sure as he could feel the sand gritting beneath the soles of his shoes as he made his way along the boardwalk.

In the summer months that he'd worked for the town, he had come across at least half a dozen runaways. Kids he'd tangled with when they'd become so desperate that they'd broken the law, a few he'd been able to help. Every single one of them exhibited the same classic characteristics—they were skittish, evasive, edgy, and distrustful. And most of them could stretch the truth like a heavy duty rubber band, rarely considering the potential snapback.

Yesterday morning, he'd seen a clear juxtaposition in Dina's behavior; she'd been warm and smiling, openly appreciative of his offer of breakfast, yet she'd become hesitant and even shifty whenever he'd attempted to ask her questions that even came close to being of a personal nature. Despite several discreet approaches, he had been unsuccessful in learning her full name. Hell, he wasn't even certain the first name she'd given him was real. And he'd caught her in one out-and-out lie.

However, as cagy as she'd acted, Dina was unlike the runaways he'd dealt with in the past—teens who had little or no adult supervision in their lives, or had taken exception to curfews or other rules laid down for them and had felt the sudden urge to revolt, or had been mistreated and felt desperate, or myriad other reasons. Dina was obviously an adult. Mature. Grown-up.

Fully ripe.

He cleared his throat, shoving the inappropriate thought aside.

He'd studied her closely while they had eaten together. Her beautiful face... Yes, he'd noticed. He'd had to have been as dead and mummified as Tutankhamun not to become mesmerized by those enticing green eyes, not to experience an itch to trail his fingers over her long, thick, copper-colored hair.

He gazed out at the ocean, zipping up his leather jacket to his chin as he shook off the weird warmth curling in his belly.

Focus, damn it.

If he had to guess, he'd say Dina was in her mid to late twenties. Although she was much older than the customary runaway-type he was used to dealing with, that didn't mean he shouldn't help her. She *was* in some kind of trouble. He sensed it. Since she'd landed in Ocean City, he was determined to find out more about her.

The door of the café swung open and he stepped inside, reveling in the warmth, enjoying the homey scents of bacon and coffee as his gaze scanned the room. Cathy stood behind the counter, and he nodded a greeting. The otherwise empty kitchen area made his heart sink.

"Morning, Gav," Cathy called. "Coffee?"

"In a to-go cup, if you don't mind," he told her. "How are you today?"

"Couldn't be better." Steam wafted from the pot when she poured.

"So Dina didn't show?"

Cathy set the coffee carafe back on the burner. "Not yet."

He pulled out his wallet and set a couple of dollar bills on the counter, then casually asked, "Think she will?"

"No reason why she wouldn't." She capped the cup. "Yesterday afternoon, she talked as if she was coming in. She seemed really grateful for the job. But—" she shrugged, "—you know how it goes."

"Yeah, no guarantees." He paused a moment, then said, "She was awfully careful with everything she said yesterday."

Cathy nodded. "I noticed that, too. I need for her to fill out her employment papers, but she ended up taking them with her. Gave the excuse of wanting to take her time and do it right."

Classic evasive behavior. Then again, Dina might be the conscientious type who wants to get it right.

Quietly, he told Cathy, "I hope I'm wrong, but I think she might be homeless."

"Oh?" Cathy absently straightened the sash of the apron she wore.

"I met her over at the pharmacy," Gav said. "She had a big plastic bag with a bar of soap, a wash cloth, toothbrush, and a tube of toothpaste. I think she was cleaning herself up in the rest room over there."

"Poor thing." Cathy reached for a cleaning cloth that sat on the counter.

"And she told me she was staying at the Princess Bayside."

Cathy cocked her head. "But—"

"Exactly. They're closed for the winter."

With a sigh, Cathy began wiping down the counter. "I guess I'll find out the truth when she turns those papers in today. I need a name, address, and phone number if I'm to get her on the books."

"*If* she brings them."

Again, Cathy nodded, murmuring, "If she shows up."

Just as a dark, sinking was settling in Gav's gut, the front door was flung open, and he swiveled around.

"Morning!" Dina sang the greeting, looking like a race-walker, arms pumping and out of breath. "Sorry I'm late. I had to walk most of the way. I don't know the bus schedule yet. Hey, Gav. How ya doing?"

She sailed by him, swinging her leopard-print backpack off her shoulders as she hurried into the kitchen.

"No harm done," Cathy called over her shoulder.

When Dina returned, she'd donned a white apron and was tying it snuggly around her waist. She grinned up at Gav. "What? No pancakes today?"

He took in her sparkling green eyes, that bright smile. It might be winter just outside that front door, but in here it was like springtime. Fresh. Joyful.

Geez, he silently swore. He never knew he could be such a sap.

"Not today." He lifted his cup. "Just coffee. I've got to get to work." Now that he'd seen Dina, the anxiety in his gut subsided to a tolerable level. "Thanks. I hope both you ladies have a good day."

He was a few feet from the door when he stopped short. "Hey, Dina." He turned. "We still on for this evening?"

"You bet we are." Her smile beamed. "We've got toys to collect."

CHAPTER FOUR

Gav took a long draw from the straw sticking out of the top of his lemonade cup. Then he set the drink next to the bag of food on the table. "So what are you going to ask Santa to bring you this Christmas?"

The question struck Dina as funny as she stood by the table. She parted her lips to speak, but he lifted his palm.

"Wait, let me guess," he said. "Something gold and glittery. Earrings, maybe. Or a diamond necklace."

"Nah." She slipped out of her coat and hung it on the back of her chair, and then she sat down across from him. "Santa hasn't come to visit me in years. Even if he did, jewelry isn't my thing." She shook her head at the look on his face. "Now don't go feeling sorry for me. I get gifts. Just not from Santa." She chuckled, tilting her head a fraction. "He doesn't come to your house either, does he?"

"Okay, you got me." He pulled their burgers from the bag. "But what if you could have anything? Anything you could think of?"

She plucked up an errant fry that had fallen onto the table. "Anything? Hmmm." She munched and swallowed. "I guess I'd have to wish for all the hungry people in the world to be fed. Or the homeless to be housed. Or everyone who needed a job to find employment."

"Ah." He nodded as he pulled his dinner out of the paper bag. "Now that's one selfless, altruistic, grown-up Christmas list if I ever heard one."

Dina refused to be ruffled by his teasing. "Well, it's hard to want frivolous things when there are so many people in need, you know?"

"I do, and I agree." He grinned. "But I wouldn't say no if I found a box of soft licorice in my stocking."

"Licorice, huh?" Her voice dropped to a whisper. "My favorite is dark chocolate covered caramels."

She watched him unwittingly rub his hands together, as if he were taking a moment to relish the thought of the dinner he was about to eat. He looked like a big kid caught up in a moment of excited anticipation and she thought it was cute.

"Speaking of people in need," he said, lifting his eyes to hers, "I can't believe how many toys we collected." He peeled back the aluminum foil that encased his hamburger. "You are amazing! My trunk and back seat are stuffed."

Dina settled herself in her seat and set her napkin on her thigh. "What I loved were all those promises of more."

"And money! When they didn't have toys to offer, *they gave money*, Dina."

She laughed at his incredulity. He'd actually scoffed at her when she'd suggested they go into every local business that was open and ask for help. Gav hadn't seen the point of going into a jewelry store or a t-shirt shop when they were looking for toy donations. She had flipped her hair over her shoulder and jokingly called him a rookie.

"It never dawned on me to go into small

businesses to ask for help. I thought my best bet was sticking to the bigger department stores. There aren't that many of them in town, but it made sense to me that they'd have more of what I needed."

"Why didn't you ask your co-workers?" she asked. "Surely, they'd have given you some advice."

"And risk being razzed into next year because I don't know how to collect toys?"

She laughed at the horror on his face. "The kids, Gav," she reminded him. "The teasing would have been worth it for the kids."

They'd started at the north end of town, stopping at every single business that was open. The Christmas season could be stressful for some people, but the spirit of giving seemed to infect everyone during the holidays. Nearly all the owners and managers they'd talked to had given something toward Gav's cause, even if it had been just a few dollars.

The sky had turned full-on dark when Gav suggested they stop at Five Guys for burgers and fries. When he'd shrugged out of his jacket and tossed it on the neighboring chair, she couldn't help but notice how the waffle fabric of his cotton shirt hugged his broad chest and narrow waist.

She'd purposefully focused her attention on pulling out her chair and taking off her own coat. The bright dining room was filled with the succulent scents of beef and onions, bacon and frying grease; comfort foods that made her stomach growl.

"We collected a lot of small items tonight," she said. "The little gifts mean a lot more effort, but they add up really fast."

"They do," he agreed. He took a sip of his soda. "A few more evenings like this, and I'll have all the toys I need. What toys aren't donated, I'll buy with the cash donations." A different kind of appreciation lit his dark gaze as he murmured, "And I can apply all this experience when I collect toys next Christmas."

The admiration resonating in his words and in his beautiful brown eyes filled Dina with warm pleasure.

Just then a woman came through the side entrance, a little girl close on her heels. The child looked to be six or seven years old. Her coarse-textured hair had been neatly sectioned and secured in multiple pigtails held with brightly colored elastic bands. Her large eyes shined with excitement. Her skin was as smooth and dark as polished rosewood. The girl's gaze landed on Dina, and Dina smiled.

Gav called out, "Hi, Mrs. Johnston. Hey, Charlie."

The woman nodded in greeting and the girl waved, offering Gav a huge grin as they trudged toward the counter to make their order.

Dina turned back to the brown bag that held her meal, finally reaching inside and pulling out her burger.

"Her name's Charlene," Gav offered. "But she goes by Charlie." Lowering his voice, he added, "She's one of my kids."

"She'll be getting toys?"

He nodded. "I've been worried that we wouldn't be able to give to everyone on the list, but I think it's going to be all right."

His grateful gaze settled on her for a long moment, and her heart thudded.

The woman and her beautiful daughter sat on the far side of the dining room. The girl offered a non-stop commentary.

"This smells so good, Mama. The bun is *warm*. Those are called sesame seeds, Mama. Did you know that? Is there such a thing as a sesame plant? If I put some in the garden, can we grow a sesame plant? Is there ketchup on it? Can I have extra ketchup? You know how much I like ketchup."

"Hush now, Charlie, and eat. We have to go home and get started on your homework."

"You wanna share with me, Mama?"

Dina glanced over and saw that their only purchase had been a small burger. No French fries, no drinks.

Gav slipped out his chair. "Mrs. Johnston, can I buy you a hamburger?"

"Oh, thank you, but no. To tell you the truth, I'm too tired to eat. Been on these feet all day."

"Are you sure? I don't mind. It'll only take a minute to—"

"Thank you, but no." The woman's spine straightened and her chin raised a fraction.

Gav let it go, but then he turned his attention to the child. "Charlie, I made a mistake and ordered too many fries. Could you take some of these off my hands?"

The girl gave a delighted gasp. "Mama! He has too many fries. Can we have some, Mama? You don't want Officer Thomas to waste any of his fries, right?" Then she looked at Gav. "Do they have ketchup on 'em? I love ketchup on my fries."

Dina watched Gav hesitate until the woman offered him a weary nod. He snatched up his bag and carried it across the room.

"They don't have ketchup on them yet," he told Charlie. "You see, I'm a dipper. So I don't squirt it all over like some people do."

"Oooo, can I be a dipper, too?"

Gav laughed, and the sound of it made Dina smile.

"Sure," he said. "Let me grab you some ketchup from the counter. Be right back."

Charlie grinned over at Dina. "We've been to see the Festival of Lights. Have you seen the lights? They're beautiful."

"I haven't," Dina admitted.

"You need to go. Over at Northside Park. Just down the street. Everyone should see them." Charlie took a bite of her hamburger and chewed. "We couldn't ride on the tram. It cost too much."

"Hush now, and eat," her mother scolded.

Not waiting for the ketchup, Charlie stuffed a fry into her mouth. "But we walked around the outside of the fence. We could see almost everything. Couldn't we, Mama?"

"Charlie, don't talk with your mouth full," her mother warned.

Gav arrived with the little white paper cup filled to the brim with ketchup.

The girl offered her thanks, then said, "I sat on Santa's lap, Officer Thomas."

"You did? What did you tell him you wanted for Christmas?"

"I want a new doll baby." Her voice went all dramatic and dreamy, as only a little girl's could. "One that looks just like me."

"What are you saying, child?" her mother asked. "Santa brought you a doll two Christmases ago."

Charlie rolled her eyes. "Mama, you know that baby's skin is white as Frosty the Snowman. Don't look nuthin' like me. Nuthin' at all."

Dina tucked her top lip between her teeth to keep the laughter bubbling inside her from spreading across her mouth in a smile. The last thing she wanted to do was insult Charlie.

"Playing with dollies," her mother said softly, "involves using your imagination."

"I know, Mama." Charlie's tone became

saturated with long-suffering. "And my 'magination is pretty good." She blinked and gazed up at Gav. "But Santa might be able to bring me a baby that looks like me. You never know unless you ask."

"That's a good point," Gav told her.

"Charlie, eat your dinner," her mother said. "And let the man get back to his hamburger before it gets cold." She smiled up at Gav. "Thank you for the French fries."

"You're welcome."

As Gav slid back into his seat, Dina heard Charlie say, "Mama, have some fries. There must be a thousand of 'em in here. Let's be dippers together."

Mrs. Johnston's chuckle sounded weary. "Charlie, hon, you are so silly." She reached into the bag and pulled out a fry. "Let me at that ketchup so I can be a dipper."

Dina leaned toward Gav and murmured, "We need to make sure there's a black baby doll under Charlie's tree on Christmas morning."

He nodded, picked up his burger, and tucked in.

Her heart felt soft as she watched him eat. Finally, she picked up her own burger, but before she took a bite she told him, "Share my fries, okay? There must be a thousand of 'em in here."

After they'd finished their meals and cleaned up their table, Dina waved goodbye to Charlie, pushed open the door of the restaurant, and led the way out into the parking lot. "Thanks for dinner," she told Gav.

"You're welcome. And thank you for helping me tonight." He zipped up his coat. "You up for another round tomorrow night?"

"Absolutely."

"At this rate," he said, "it won't take me long before I have a gift for every kid on my list. And that's great because we're supposed to have them ready to be picked up on Wednesday."

"Listen, if none of the contributors offers you an African American doll, I'll be happy to buy one for Charlie." Dina grinned as she glanced through the window at the little girl inside yammering away at her mother. "She's so cute."

"You don't need to do that. I have those cash donations. Charlie's doll will be wrapped up and waiting for her mom to pick up on Wednesday."

Dina took a few seconds to look at Gav. Softly, she told him, "So many children are going to have a happy Christmas because of this good thing you're doing."

"*We're* doing. You've been so great tonight, Dina. I mean it. I wasn't doing so well on my own."

She smiled, loving the way he made her feel.

Tilting his head, he scrubbed at the back of his neck. "After working all day," he said, "and tramping around town with me for hours, you must be dead on your feet. How about if I drop you off at, ah... your hotel?"

Dina reached to pull up the hood of her coat. Winter chilled the air, yes, but in reality, she needed a moment to think. This was as good a time as any to go ahead and rent a room. She couldn't imagine spending a third night sleeping on that concrete floor. The sleeping bag she'd bought was warm enough; however, her hip bones were no match for that cement surface.

It wouldn't hurt for him to let her off out front of the Princess Bayside. After he drove off, she'd go into the office and rent a room.

"Sure," she told him. "That sounds great. Thanks."

He went oddly quiet as they got into his car and turned the key in the ignition. A car's engine needed warming up during the cold winter months, she realized, but they hadn't been inside the restaurant very long. Yet, he sat there for an inordinate amount of time.

Finally, she asked, "What's wrong?"

Other than the sound of sparse traffic on Coastal Highway and purring of the car's engine, the night was still.

"Dina, what are you playing at?"

The pole lights high overhead cast his face in deep enough shadow that she couldn't see his expression, but she didn't like what she heard in his voice.

"Playing at?" she said. "What are you talking about?"

He sighed and raked his fingers through his hair. Then he glanced over at her. "I know you're not staying at Princess Bayside."

Her lips parted when her jaw dropped open a fraction. "Have you been following me?"

"Absolutely not."

The two words were sharp enough that, had they been a knife, they'd have made a clean, deep cut. Dina clamped her mouth shut, but her gaze never wavered from his.

Gav heaved a sigh and swiveled his head to glance out the windshield.

"Princess Bayside closes for the winter," he told her quietly. "And besides that, the first time we met you were carrying your bathroom gear. I suspected you'd cleaned yourself up in the pharmacy's restroom."

Heat flushed her face and neck. He'd found her out. And so easily, at that. She felt annoyed. At him. And herself. How could she be so stupid?

"Won't be long," she muttered, "before you're promoted to detective."

He ignored her. Then his head swiveled and his eyes clashed with hers once more. Her mouth pursed stubbornly.

"Tell me the truth, Dina," he finally demanded. "Where have you been staying?" He paused for two long, drawn out seconds before asking, "And who are you running from?"

CHAPTER FIVE

"Dina!"

She nearly jumped out of her skin at the sound of Cathy's voice. Dina released the button on the sprayer nozzle and the jet of hot water stopped, and then she whipped her head around to look at her boss.

"What?" Cathy lifted her hands in the air, palms up, her right hand clutching the towel she'd been using to wipe down the countertop. "You trying to wash the color off those dishes? They were clean five minutes ago."

"Sorry," Dina muttered, glancing down at the rack of steaming hot plates and coffee mugs.

"Are you okay? You've been pre-occupied all morning."

"I'm fine." She sighed the words, and she wasn't surprised when Cathy didn't look convinced.

Dina fisted her still-wet hand and settled it on her hip. "Cathy, you know that Gav has helped me. A lot. I mean, I wouldn't be working here if I hadn't met him. But do you think that means I have an obligation to tell him every secret I've ever had?"

Cathy's spine straightened and her jaw went tense. "You and Gav had an argument?"

"Not an argument," she admitted. "But we did have words. He's not happy with me. But he's pushing me. He wants me to tell him things I'm just not... comfortable talking about." Exhaling with a whoosh, she softly added, "Not with a cop, anyway."

"You just met him." Cathy crossed her arms, her eyebrows drawing together a fraction. "You don't have to tell him a damned thing."

That feistiness was one of the reasons Dina liked Cathy, and it made her grin. No one ever wondered what the woman was thinking. She spoke her mind, good, bad, or indifferent. The first day Dina had worked in the café, Cathy had made her wash and then rewash that first rack of dishes, plainly stating, "I won't serve food on anything but impeccably clean plates. Give it another go."

As the two women stood in the kitchen now, Cathy's shoulders eased. "I want you to know you can talk to me. If you need to. If you *want to*... I mean, if you're in some kind of trouble..."

The rest of Cathy's sentence trailed off.

Dina pursed her lips, giving herself a minute to think. She didn't want to alienate the only friends she'd made since coming to Ocean City, but neither did she want to drag them into her messy situation.

"I'll tell you the same thing I told Gav." Dina tugged the dish towel from the waistband of her apron and began patting her hands dry. "I haven't done anything wrong."

They stared at each other as silence settled between them.

Finally, Cathy said, "Alrighty then. Will you be all right here alone for a few minutes? I'm going to the store room for some supplies."

Once she was alone, Dina turned toward the rack of dishes and began unloading it. Gav's anxious face swam to the forefront of her mind.

"Where have you been staying? And who are you running from?"

Feeling like a kid caught with a stolen chocolate bar, Dina remained silent and gazed out the passenger window into the night. She watched Charlie and her mother come out of the fast food joint and trudge their way toward the bus stop out on Coastal Highway.

"Dina?"

She worried her top lip with her teeth until she feared she'd draw blood. Finally, she got up enough courage to look at him.

"Look, I'm sorry I lied to you." Although she kept her tone quiet, it seemed to reverberate in the close confines of the car's interior. "I hadn't noticed that Princess Bayside was closed. That is where I intended to stay when I finally got around to, you know, renting a room. I'm not lying about that, Gav."

Dina hoped he believed her.

"So where have you been sleeping?" he pressed.

The urge to squirm under his scrutiny hit her. Hard. Again, she looked away from him.

"Come on, Dina. Talk to me. I'm worried about you."

"You don't have to worry," she told him, biding herself a little more time.

His hand came down on the steering wheel with a thump. "Dina! Just tell me."

"Fine." The word snapped like a tree branch. "If you must know, I've been sleeping in the stairwell of a parking garage."

She stole a glance at him and the horror on his face tied her stomach into a knot of nerves.

"But it's the middle of winter."

"The temperatures are pretty mild here," she rushed to tell him. "Compared to home, anyway."

His head tilted. "And where's that?"

She ignored the question. "Besides, I have a sleeping bag. I've been warm enough."

"Damn, Dina," he said. "Don't you know that's trespassing? You could get into trouble. If you need money for a hotel room—"

"I have money," she rushed to assure him. "I don't need any money. I was merely trying to conserve my cash. There's no crime in that, is there?"

"You cannot spend another night in a parking garage. I mean it."

"I won't. I had already planned on finding a hotel room for tonight." Then she murmured, "I've been washing up as best I can, and I'm using a ton of deodorant. But I'm ready for a hot shower. And a soft bed."

They sat in the dark for a moment, heat blasting from the vent.

"I can't believe you," he finally said. "A parking garage. Geez, Dina."

She couldn't tell him, but those hours she'd spent curled up in that sleeping bag, surrounded by all that concrete block, had instilled a feeling of safety she hadn't felt since fleeing Baltimore. In that stairwell, no one knew where she was. No one. The sense of security has allowed her to let down her guard and sleep.

"I said I'd find a hotel." She hoped he'd drop the subject now that she'd told him what he'd wanted to know. But it seemed he wasn't completely satisfied.

"Tell me what you're running from."

"Gav, please leave it alone. My problems are my problems. I don't want to talk about it."

"But you're in some kind of trouble." When she didn't respond, he voice went quiet with appeal. "You can trust me, Dina. Let me help you."

The officers in Baltimore had said the very same thing. Trust us. Let us help you.

She had. And her whole life had been upended.

Gav Thomas was a perfectly nice person. He'd helped her without giving it a second thought. He was kind and compassionate. She didn't doubt his trustworthiness.

But he was a cop. An officer of the law. If he were to learn the circumstances that had forced her to flee, he'd be obligated to contact the Baltimore City Police Department.

Dina wasn't going back there. She wasn't putting her life into anyone's hands.

Shifting on the seat, she stared into his eyes. "I will tell you this, and only this: I have done nothing wrong." She paused long enough to let that information sink in. "That's going to have to be good enough."

He hadn't been happy with her. She'd been able to tell by the set of his jaw, the tension in his shoulders. He'd promised not to ask her any more questions, but only after she'd insisted on it. He'd driven her to a motel he knew to be open year round, and on the way, he'd lectured her about being aware of her surroundings, about keeping her doors locked, about walking with her head up rather than looking down at the sidewalk or her cell phone.

She desperately wanted to assure him that no

one knew she was in Ocean City. But doing so would only encourage more questions, so she just listened to him talk and nodded her thanks at each piece of advice.

The last of the thick ceramic coffee mugs were all lined up, clean and ready for the next customers, when Cathy returned to the kitchen with a large container of ground coffee.

"Hey, before I forget," Cathy told her, "count out the tips for the day and take your half. Put my share in my office on the desk, okay?"

"I'll get right on it."

"After that—" Cathy scanned the kitchen "—I guess you can go for the day."

"Right." Dina reached around and untied her apron.

"And Dina," she said. "Gav is one of the good ones."

Dina looked at the apron she folded, nodding.

"Oh, one more thing," Cathy said.

Dina looked questioningly at Cathy.

"If you want a paycheck," the woman told her, "I have to have that paperwork so I can get you on the books."

Dina offered a smile. She wasn't sure what she

was going to do about that pesky paperwork problem. She was learning that remaining incognito was not as easy as it sounded.

CHAPTER SIX

The last of the Christmas toys had been collected, and Dina and Gav spent the better part of the early evening at the station house with other off-duty officers and volunteers, wrapping and labeling gifts, and filling stockings with pencils, crayons, candy canes, and other little odds and ends that had been collected. Each stocking also contained a large, fragrant navel orange, a last minute donation from a local grocer. A palpable energy reverberated in the big conference room.

At seven o'clock, the magic hour, parents began arriving to collect the toys and filled stockings that had been collected for their children. Happy holiday music filled the air, and the buzz of cheerful voices added to the excitement.

All the officers and volunteers were kept busy loading bags with gifts and a stocking. Every so often, Dina would catch Gav staring at her and they'd exchange smiles. There was nothing more gratifying than knowing you were doing a good deed that would make so many children happy.

There were givers in this world, and there were takers. Gav was clearly a giver. Over the course of the evenings that she'd spent with Gav, seeing him interact with little Charlie and her mother, witnessing how seriously he worked at making the Giving Project a success, Dina had discovered Gav's giving spirit. It had been an admirable sight to behold.

Dina handed over a bag of gifts and stockings to an exceptionally grateful man.

"You have no idea what this means to me." His eyes glittered with moisture. "No idea what this is going to mean to my boys."

"Happy Christmas to you," Dina told him. Emotion balled in her throat.

From the corner of her eye, she saw a young woman approach Gav.

"Officer Thomas?" the woman said. "I'm from The Dispatch. The Chief told me you were in charge of the Christmas Giving Project this year. Do you mind if I ask you a few questions?"

"Don't mind at all." Gav handed Dina the clipboard he'd been holding so she could continue to help the parents who were waiting.

Dina turned and nearly ran into a young man intent on getting to Gav.

"Officer Thomas," the guy said, stepping around Dina as if she wasn't there. "I'm from OC Today. Can I talk to you for a minute? I'm doing a story on your project. Lots of people here." He flashed a glistening white grin. "Looks like a great success."

Chatting with a reporter—even though she hadn't known the woman's occupation at the time—had been the start of all Dina's troubles back in Baltimore, so it seemed only natural for her to do a slow, inconspicuous shuffle-step to the left until there were several volunteers between her, Gav, and the journalists.

Since the time Dina had been a young child, she'd been taught that helping those less fortunate than she was, was not only the right thing to do, it was a civic responsibility. Volunteering for events just like Gav's Giving Project, Dina had learned, not only cultivated a deep sense of well-being, but the experiences had allowed her to meet many interesting people, had helped to give her a sense of purpose and being needed, and had also developed her social skills and honed her organizing abilities. She'd given of her time and often even her money, but she'd always received something for the effort.

Every person who picked up gifts here tonight expressed a deep and abiding gratitude. And Dina felt thankful for the opportunity to help. *This* was one of the true meanings of Christmas. This project could only strengthen the community, make it closer, more tight-knit, and it pleased her to be a part of it.

A few minutes later, the female reporter who had been interviewing Gav approached her.

"Dina?" the woman said. "The Chief told us you were instrumental in making the project a success. Can I ask you a few questions?" Without waiting for a response, she said, "Would you tell me your full name? Do you live in Ocean City?"

"I'm just a regular volunteer," Dina told her. "Just like everyone else."

"But you are Dina, right?" The reported looked disconcerted. "The Chief said—"

"I'm no one important," Dina insisted. "Trust me."

Hoping the woman would go away, Dina focused on the next parent to approach the gift table.

"Mrs. Johnston!" Dina beamed. "You probably don't remember me..."

"Oh, but I do." The woman's midnight gaze twinkled. "We met at Five Guys."

Dina nodded. "Wait right there a second. I know right where Charlie's gifts are." In a flash she was back, handing over the doll she had painstakingly wrapped herself along with the stocking brimming with items that would make any little girl smile on Christmas morning.

"This is just what Charlie wanted." Dina gave the woman a little wink.

"Aw, you didn't have to go to such trouble." She accepted the gift as if Dina were handing her a bar of solid gold.

Several bright flashes went off at the same time, and Dina blinked before looking up to see at least two photographers pointing cameras at her. The reporter hovered just a few feet away. Clearly, she was about to make another approach.

"My daughter sure will be happy when she opens it. Thank you very much," Mrs. Johnston said. "You have a Merry Christmas now. Please tell Officer Thomas I appreciate all he's done."

"I'll tell him."

Just as the second reporter joined the first, Dina told the volunteer closest to her that she needed a break.

She slipped out of the nearest exit, searched around the well-lit, empty hallways until she found a restroom, and then locked herself in a cubicle. Leaning against the green metal wall, she gazed up at the ceiling.

"You are *not* very good at this laying low business, are you?" she whispered to herself.

CHAPTER SEVEN

Dina lingered first in the ladies room and then in the parking lot, where she'd strolled around, hoping to avoid any further attention. By the time she made her way back inside, the reporters had left and the event was gearing down to the point that the volunteers were cleaning up.

"There you are." Gav swiped his forearm across his brow. "I was afraid you might have left."

"No," she said. "I just needed a little fresh air." She noticed that the extra tables were being broken down and set on a large wheeled trolley. "I'd better grab my backpack before it's in someone's way."

He nodded, falling into step beside her. "I'm really happy with how everything turned out. The police department got lots of good media coverage tonight."

"I saw you talking to the reporters."

"WBOC News showed up with a camera crew." He looked quite pleased with himself.

"You're going to be on TV?"

Gav shrugged. "Dunno. They interviewed the Chief and they also talked to me. But you never know. My thirty seconds of fame could easily get deleted."

"True, but I don't think that'll happen. You'll make more interesting airtime than your boss." She leaned toward him and softly said, "You're much better looking than he is."

Amusement twisted his lips. "Yeah, yeah, yeah. Whatever."

His "aw, shucks" reaction made her laugh.

"Listen," he said, "when we finish up here can I take you some place?"

"Where?"

As soon as the one word question passed her lips, she spied her backpack on the floor. The flap was open and some of the contents had spilled out.

"Oh, no." She hurried over, leaned down onto her knees to grab up her wallet, and she opened it. No money seemed to be missing, and her credit cards and driving license were right where they belonged. She closed the wallet with a relieved sigh.

One of the volunteers, the woman Dina had been standing next to before leaving the room, called out from a few yards away where she was stacking some folding chairs. "Your bag must have fallen off the chair. Mighta' gotten kicked around a bit. I didn't see it happen, but once I saw your things there on the floor, I've been watching so no one messed with your stuff. If you didn't come back, I planned to hand everything over to the Chief."

"Thanks for keeping an eye out. I appreciate it." Dina picked up the backpack and tossed her wallet, lip gloss, a travel packet of tissues, and her hair brush back inside. Gav had bent to retrieve an ink pen, a couple of hair clips, and several receipts and handed them to her.

"So what do you say?" he asked. "Will you go with me?"

"Sure."

After finishing up at the station, Gav took Dina to a nearby fast food place and picked up two cups of hot chocolate at the drive through window. He handed one to her and placed his in the cup holder in the center console.

"Just the smell of chocolate makes me salivate," she said.

"It's good stuff." He pulled out onto Coastal Highway and headed south. "The Aztecs and the Mayans thought chocolate was a gift from the gods. The Greeks called it the food of the gods." He grinned at her. "I wrote a paper for my high school chemistry class."

Nervous energy began to tickle her insides. Dina chose to think it was caused by the anticipation of sipping the delicious drink she held in her hand rather than the smile he'd just graced her with.

"I could tell you all about the chemical make up of the bitter alkaloids in the cacao beans, and how theobromine is slightly water-soluble and has the same sort of effect on the human nervous system as caffeine, but that doesn't sound nearly as romantic as gifts from gods, now, does it?"

The question—or maybe it was the sultry sound of his voice—made her a bit breathless, so she lifted the cup to her lips to take a small sip so she wouldn't have to answer him.

He made a left and drove down a short side street toward the ocean. When the asphalt ran out, he kept the car creeping forward along the wide, hard-packed dune crossing, and stopped at the apex of the mound.

Sand spread out before them like a carpet. The nearly full moon looked huge in the ink black sky, and for a moment, Dina forgot all about the tickle in her stomach, the conversation they'd been having, even the taste of the hot chocolate on her tongue.

"Oh, my gosh," she whispered, leaning forward a few inches. "Look at that moon. It's so fat. And bright." Suddenly she felt as giddy as a kid. She turned to Gav. "Can we get out? I want to go out onto the beach."

"That's exactly what I was hoping for."

She gazed out the windshield again. "This is what you wanted to show me?"

"Mm-hm. The full moon's a couple days off, but I couldn't wait any longer. I wanted you to see this."

They took their hot chocolate and trudged

across the sand toward the ocean's edge. The waves crashed against the shore in a calming, rhythmical cadence. The barren beach stretched north and south, and although the sky was full dark, the moon illuminated the coastline in a bluish, radiant glow.

"It's beautiful, Gav. Can we sit?"

"That sounds good." He glanced around for a slight mound. "The sand is probably cold, but it's dry."

They settled themselves, their shoulders pressing together. Dina inhaled the mingling scents of rich chocolate in her cup, his woodsy cologne, and the salty tang of the sea water. She sipped her drink.

"So that talk in the car," she finally said, "about your chemistry paper... does that mean you were interested in science?"

"Not really. I'm sure I mentioned before that I always wanted to be a police officer like my dad." He laced his fingers around his Styrofoam cup. "But chemistry was necessary if I wanted to get into college. I finished a four year degree in law enforcement at Penn State, and then I was accepted into the police academy."

He lifted the hot chocolate and took a drink, then he asked, "How about you? Did you go to college?"

"I was only able to finish a two year degree," she said. "At... a local community college. My mom didn't have the money for more than that, and I didn't want to go into debt." She lifted one shoulder. "Besides that, I needed to work. My mom needed the help. Continues to need the help."

Although Gav remained silent, she could see he was curious.

The sadness in her sigh was as familiar as an old friend; it was the same sigh that issued from her each time she talked about her father. "My dad died when I was just a kid. I barely remember him. Mom remarried when I was ten. George has a... weakness. For alcohol. He does what he can. Works when and where he can. He can go dry for days, weeks even. But *The Taste*, that's how he describes it, always gets the better of him, sooner or later."

Gav's brown eyes studied her until she wanted to squirm.

"I don't want you to think he's a bad person. He's sweet and kind. He loves my mom. And me."

She lifted her shoulders. "He just has a problem. A lot of families have problems."

She didn't mean to sound guarded or defensive or glib. She'd lived with the reality of George's drinking for the better part of fifteen years; long enough for it to have become just another thread in the fabric of her existence.

"You're right," Gav said, his tone as soft as the night sky, "a lot of people have problems."

Dina had learned long ago not to delve too deeply into explanations of George's behavior. How could she when she didn't understand his uncontrollable craving herself? An alcoholic was an alcoholic. End of discussion. You deal with the situations when they crop up, and then you move on.

"It didn't take long for me to learn just how far my Associates Degree was going to take me," she said. "I ended up taking a job as a waitress. It was hard work, but it was honest work. It wasn't long before I was promoted to hostess, and then a couple years ago I started managing the staff. I'm sort of the staff manager and the assistant manager now."

"Good for you," he murmured. "Working your way up to management level."

Dina gazed out at the undulating ocean. "Believe me, the job wasn't all that. There was plenty of grunt work involved. And I still had to wait tables when we were short on staff."

"You've started talking in the past tense. You're not working there anymore?"

She looked down at the white plastic lid that covered her cup. Little whiffs of chocolaty vapor continued to escape.

"I'm not sure," she told him quietly. "I had to take some time off."

When she turned her gaze up to his face, she could plainly see there were questions rolling through his head.

"Gav," she quietly warned, "you promised not to prod me."

"Okay, okay." He leaned into her slightly. "But you sure don't make it easy. The tiny bit you're telling me about yourself... You make me want to prod you."

Laughter bubbled in Dina's chest. She pressed her lips together and did her best to keep from sniggering at him. Arching her brows, she just looked at him and asked, "Did you really just say that?"

"Oh, hell," he muttered. "I am not going to let you embarrass me, Dina. That's not what I meant." He twisted at the waist and set the cup of hot chocolate on the sand near his hip, and then he turned back around to face her. "But since you brought it up, does that mean you feel it, too? This *thing*?"

Her first impulse was to continue to tease him about the naughty connotations of his choice of words, but his gaze had turned quite serious.

"You're special," he said. "I felt it that very first day we met. Out in the parking lot at the pharmacy. There was a... a... connection or something. I wanted to know you. Wanted to *get* to know you. Yet at the same time, I felt I already *did* know you. It was the oddest sensation. One I wanted to explore. That's the main reason why I invited you to breakfast. You had to have noticed."

He took her free hand in his, splayed it out onto his rock-hard thigh and began tracing small circles on her skin with the pad of his index finger.

"And then you did the most amazing thing. You agreed to help me collect up toys for the project."

Dina couldn't decide which was more delicious; the light touch of his fingers on her hand, or the sound of the awe in his voice. Both were as provocative as warm satin brushing against bare skin.

"It was crazy," he continued. "Why would you do that? Why would you help a total stranger?"

She kept her gaze locked on the movement of his fingers on the back of her hand and wrist. It was as if the nerves directly beneath the skin he slowly caressed were directly linked to some secret, erogenous place deep inside her. Though there was a chill in the air, she felt overly warm, and even with all this fresh air swirling around them, she found it difficult to breathe.

I don't know, she wanted to answer him. But she couldn't seem to form the words.

He reached up and tucked a gentle knuckle under her chin, guiding her face and her gaze to his. The fervor in his dark eyes overwhelmed her.

"You felt it, right?" he whispered. He took her cup from her and blindly set it near his. "I can't imagine that you didn't."

Gav leaned toward her, and she realized he meant to kiss her.

"I don't know," she was finally able to murmur. The words sounded winded, as if she'd sprinted a mile in the sand. "I... I really don't. But I do know we shouldn't do this."

His mouth curled into a languid smile. "But you're not going to let that stop us."

He hovered there, mere inches from her face, giving her time, she guessed, to decide what it was she wanted to do. Desire spiraled through her like liquid heat, relaxing her muscles, melting her bones, and without another thought, she surrendered to the irresistible lure of his lips and leaned toward him.

Their kiss was tentative at first, and Dina let her eyelids slide shut as she savored the sensations.

Feverish heat.

Soft yet firm.

Velvety.

Moist.

A hint of sweetness.

And chocolate.

The light friction of his tongue against her bottom lip urged her to open herself to him. She met his tongue with hers, and their passion grew bolder, needier. His arms encircled her, and she let her hands slide across his back, the temperature contrast startling her—the iciness of his leather coat beneath her palms and the fire of his mouth on hers, hot as mid-summer sunshine.

Their breathing both quickened and intensified, the sound momentarily drowning out the pounding of the surf. Her pulse throbbed thickly and her heart thudded like a bass drum.

The kiss ended with a dozen or more tiny nips, tastes, pecks, both of them reluctant to pull apart. Finally, they sat there, side by side, silent and stupefied. Breathless. His arm remained draped along her back, his blazing fingers tucked between her upper thigh and the sand.

Finally, he said, "I've never felt like this."

She turned her head to look into his handsome face. His gaze held a dreamy quality that pleased her to the point that she thought her joy would burst her lungs like overfilled balloons.

"I mean, I've dated plenty, of course. I even had a couple of serious relationships."

Her mouth cocked wryly and her brows crept up her forehead.

"Okay," he quickly revised, "a few. I *am* thirty years old."

"Hey, I didn't say a word."

"You didn't have to." He chuckled. "That orneriness in your eyes said it all."

The rumble of his laugh made her want to round her shoulders and curl into him... lie down with him right here in the sand and stare up at that big, fat, gorgeous moon.

"I'm serious, Dina," he said. "I want you to understand. I've never experienced this... this... I don't even know what to call it. It's potent. Powerful. Amazing."

She watched the movement of his throat when he swallowed, and she reached up and slid her fingers along his neck.

"I'll tell you... it's... it's—" his head shook slowly as he worked to find the words "—it's like I've spent my life meeting crones, and I've finally bagged a... a... I don't know. *A vixen.*"

"Gavin Thomas!" She couldn't help but laugh at his explanation. "Those women would not appreciate being called crones." She yanked lightly on the collar of his coat. "And I'll have you know being called a vixen isn't much better."

"What do you mean? A vixen is beautiful. And bewitching." He looked over her shoulder a moment, nodding. Then he stared deeply into her eyes. "That's how I feel, Dina. Bewitched. By you."

"But you hardly know me."

He looked deeply into her eyes. "But I do."

She didn't respond. She was too busy tamping down the trepidation that sprouted like a seed. It coiled and twisted inside her like a slow-growing but persistent vine. Sitting here with Gav was a mistake. She should not be sharing lingering kisses with this man. And it was nothing but bullheadedness that had her wanting to hold on to these delightful moments just a while longer.

They went quiet, simply enjoying the sound of the waves and the moon hanging over the ocean like a heavy-headed flower.

Out of the corner of her eye, she saw Gav's chin lift.

"My name's not Gavin," he said.

His brown hair looked glossy under the moonlight as she silently watched him and waited.

He inhaled deeply, a small smile playing at the corners of his mouth.

"I have no idea why I'm about to tell you this." He placed his fist on the sand and shifted so he could more easily look at her. "I haven't willingly admitted this for years. But here goes." His nostrils flared slightly as he steeled himself with a deep inhalation. "My given name is Gavreel."

Her lips parted in silent surprise. "You're named after the Angel of Peace?"

The question clearly astonished him. "How the hell did you know that?"

She offered him a smug smile. "I know lots of stuff." Then she chuckled.

"My mom is a devout Catholic." He brushed his palms together slowly as if to remove some pesky granules of sand. "She knows the name of every saint. Every angel. She can recite a hundred different prayers. For a hundred different situations."

One of Dina's shoulders lifted a smidge. "Well, when you have so many family members in harm's way every day," she said, "praying to saints and angels sounds completely understandable to me."

He rested his elbow on his bent knee. "I have to admit that I'm more than a little surprised. Firstly, because you know the name of the Angel of Peace. And, secondly, that you evidently don't find it at all weird that I was named after an angel." His head tilted. "Were you raised in a Catholic home, too?"

She shook her head. "My mom isn't what you'd call religious. She's more... spiritual. In a New Age kind of way." She ended the sentence on an upward note, more like a question than a statement, in an effort to gauge his response to the phrase she'd used.

So many people were put off by what they perceived as mystical, or cultish, or, yes, even wacky. She'd heard it all over the years, experienced all manner of reaction from friends, family, and strangers, everything from curiosity to fear to outright repulsion. Dina might not have deep convictions when it came to any particular religion or sacred practice, but neither would she stand by and let anyone ridicule her mother's beliefs.

"Religious or not," Gav said, a grin tweaking his tone, "if your mother taught you about Gavreel, I'm sure my mom would heartily approve."

His easy smile and his comment helped Dina to relax enough to admit, "Fear not, child of the heavenly realm. I was named after an angel, too."

A frown creased the tiny area between his dark brows and his chin drew in sharply. "Are you joking?"

Her mouth flattened and she shook her head. "Absolutely not. My mom told me that, as a child, she was called flighty and silly. She said she took that to mean her parents and teachers and most of her classmates thought she was stupid." Dina paused. "She's not. Let me assure you. But unfortunately that's how she felt about herself. So when I was born, she wanted to give me all the help that she felt she didn't get... so she named me after the Angel of Learning."

Gazing out at the moonlight glittering on the water, Dina said, "Lot of good it did me. I didn't have the money to earn my bachelor's degree."

"Well, there are plenty of other ways to learn besides college, you know."

She smiled. "Yeah. You're right."

Silence enveloped them like a cozy, warm blanket, not in the least awkward, and Dina thought she wouldn't mind sitting right here all night long.

Finally, Gav glanced over at her. "What the hell are the odds? I mean, it's incredible that your mother and mine both named their kids after angels. It's freakishly coincidental, don't you think?"

Dina sat there a moment, looking at his face—his mouth, his nose, his hair, his eyes—astonished by the attraction she felt for him and as bewildered as he by the commonality of their angelic namesakes.

"Well," she told him quietly, "if Mom was here, she'd tell you there's no such thing as a coincidence."

CHAPTER EIGHT

Flat, steel gray clouds darkened the sky and an icy mist sharpened the air to a razor's edge that froze the fingers and reddened the cheeks of anyone who braved the elements for longer than a few minutes; however, nothing could dampen the spirits of those Dina met on her way to work Christmas Eve morning. The bus driver played lively music over the sound system, people on the bus, the streets, and the boardwalk smiled, even Al and Lyle, the two "regulars" at the café who often engaged in verbal fisticuffs over some topic or other, offered her a pleasant greeting.

"It's cold out there, huh?" Cathy said as she

watched Dina hang up her backpack and coat on the hook in the closet off the kitchen area.

"My fingers are like icicles." Dina rubbed her palms together to create a little friction.

"You'll warm up soon enough." Cathy used a silicone spatula to transfer the tuna salad she'd just made into a glass container. "Listen, do you think you could handle things this afternoon?"

As soon as Cathy found out Dina had experience working in a restaurant, Dina's job had expanded a little more each day. She continued to bus tables and wash dishes, of course, but she also made and served coffee, acted as sous chef, and she filled and served orders during the busier lunch hour. Not that the café was ever really busy; half a dozen or so customers usually arrived around noon. But Dina was happy to help Cathy make sandwiches or ladle the soup-of-the-day into bowls so that people spent less time waiting to eat.

"I'm going to a party tonight and I'm not quite ready," Cathy explained. "Getting together at The Loon with my friends is a Christmas Eve tradition." She pointed toward the ceiling.

The Lonely Loon was the name of the B&B located directly above the café. From the things

Cathy had said, Dina knew the B&B upstairs and the sweet shop next door were owned by two of Cathy's good friends.

"Sure. I don't mind closing up for you."

"Every Christmas, Heather goes out of her way to make a delicious meal," Cathy told Dina. "This year we're all contributing, and I'm hoping to wow her and Sara. I found a recipe for paella with scallops and artichokes. And my dessert contribution is going to be roasted pears with espresso mascarpone cream. Sara will bake something orgasmic, I'm sure, but I'm going to try to give her a run for her money."

Dina thought about the empty hotel room where she'd be spending Christmas Eve, probably singing carols all alone between slices of pizza.

"Oh, my." Dina stopped long enough to swallow. "The espresso mascarpone sounds so good."

Delight lit Cathy's face. "I'm going to show them all this year." She sealed the container of tuna with a plastic lid. "Hey, would you like to come tonight? You could bring Gav."

"He drove to Cumberland to be with his family,"

Dina said. "He has to work tomorrow, so he's having his Christmas with them today."

"You come, then." Cathy crossed the kitchen and tucked the container into the fridge, and then she closed the door. "Unless you already have plans."

Dina smiled as she shook her head. As she put on the white apron, she pondered that greasy pizza that would surely have her name on it, and then she imagined the paella and roasted pears and who knew what other "orgasmic" dessert she *could* be enjoying if she'd allow herself to forget about the problems she was running away from for just one evening.

"No, no plans," she finally murmured. "But I hate to intrude..."

"Oh, stop." Cathy waved her off. "We'd love to have you."

Hesitating for a moment, Dina said, "Could I think about it?"

"Absolutely."

"Yo," Al called out. "If you ladies are working this morning—"

Dina and Cathy both turned to the two men sitting at the counter.

"We could use some more cream over here," Lyle finished the sentence.

If there were a Loyal Customer trophy to be awarded, Al and Lyle would win it, hands down. The men arrived promptly each morning and stayed until well after lunch. Dina could have sworn that she'd heard them switch their positions often on any number of topics—politics, the economy, parenting, global warming—all for the sake of the debate. Some days they left the café in a huff at each other, but they always showed up the next morning.

"Just hold your horses, gentleman," Cathy groused at them.

She often gave them a hard time, but Dina knew her boss was fond of both men.

"I'm on it." Dina turned toward the refrigerator.

She'd already begun filling the cream pitcher on the counter when Cathy called out, "Oh, and there's no need for you to continue to drag your heels about that paperwork." She picked up a boiled egg from the bowl at her elbow and began tapping it on the counter. "You know, now your name is out there."

"What?" Dina's head whipped around so

quickly, she splashed cream on her hand and the counter. "Shoot." She snatched a napkin from the holder and began mopping up the mess.

"The paperwork," Cathy said. "I told you I can't pay you until—"

"No. I mean, yes. I mean, what do you mean my name is out there?"

"Here, sweetheart," Al said, tapping his index finger on the local paper sitting near his coffee mug. "Dina Griffith is what I read. There's a nice picture of you and everything."

"But that's impossible." Cream dripped down Dina's wrist and up into her sleeve.

"I watched it on WBOC this morning," Lyle added. "While I was shaving."

"But I didn't talk to the reporters, or anyone from WPOC."

"WBOC," Lyle corrected.

"Who has a television in the bathroom?" Al shook his head.

"It's not *in* the bathroom, you idiot," Lyle groused. "It's in the bedroom." Then the old guy's watery eyes shifted to Dina. "There's no need to be upset, hon. The news anchor praised you, up and down. And the article was really nice, too. Tell her, Al. They only said good things, right?"

Cathy was at Dina's side, touching her shoulder. "Are you okay? You've gone a little pale. I know you said you weren't in trouble, but..."

The rest of Cathy's inquiry went unspoken.

The attention made Dina uncomfortable.

She straightened her spine and dabbed at her hand with the napkin. Looking Cathy in the eyes, she said, "I didn't do anything wrong. I mean that."

Her boss said, "I believe you."

CHAPTER NINE

Hotel rooms came in every shape and size, from grand, glitzy, and glamorous, to dinky and dingy. The room Dina had rented was somewhere in between. It was clean, comfortable and... beige. Completely monochromatic. The walls, the furniture, the bedspread, the drapes, the towels. Why hadn't she noticed it before tonight?

Probably because she hadn't spent much time here. She'd been helping Gav with his project almost every night since her arrival. And since the toys had been disbursed, she and Gav had continued to spend their evenings together; dinner and a movie, dinner and bowling, dinner and drive along the narrow, meandering roads along the moonlit bay. Her usual routine upon arriving at the hotel each evening was to take a quick shower, do a little reading, and go to sleep. She awoke early, dressed, and hurried to get to the café in time for the breakfast shift.

But she was pacing the room tonight. Twelve steps. That's what it took to go from one wall to the other. The bed took up the biggest part of the floor space. There was a simple desk and straight-backed chair.

The beige curtains were drawn tight, as they had been since she'd moved into the hotel. She hadn't gone near them. The last time she'd stayed in a rented room and had peeked out the window, what she'd seen had chilled her blood and caused her to run as fast and as hard as she could.

Besides those few moments in the pharmacy when Gav had first approached her, Dina hadn't suffered a moment of fear. There had been no need. She was away from the danger, and no one besides her mom knew where she was. But that had all changed this morning.

Her picture had been printed in the paper. The photographer had captured the gratitude sparkling in Mrs. Johnston's teary eyes, and Dina had been smiling back at the woman. Even if the image had been grainy, which it hadn't, her identity had been disclosed in the story—Dina Griffith of Bel Aire, Maryland—plain and clear for everyone to read. Law-abiding citizens, Baltimore detectives and cops, and drug dealers, alike.

"Okay, just calm down, Dina," she murmured to the empty room.

There was a huge possibility that Joe "Snag" Richardson would never find out she'd fled to Ocean City. Both of the newspapers that had carried the story that included her name were local. But the TV news station had also run the story. And that was the sticky point. Lyle said he'd seen it in the morning, and Dina had seen it herself when the segment had been repeated during the noon news today while she'd been working at the café. WBOC broadcast across the eastern shore, which included Baltimore.

Dina thought about the night the Giving Project had culminated, the people milling around, the reporters who'd tried to talk to her, her backpack open, her belongings scattered. Getting her name and hometown from her driving license would have been easy enough. Why hadn't she thought to take her backpack with her when she'd left the room?

Her thoughts cantered crazily like horses jostling for position around a dirt track.

What were the chances that Richardson had been watching the same news station at just the right time to see her image, hear her name, learn her current whereabouts?

The muffled sound of voices coming from the parking lot caught her attention. She listened for a moment, then two. Realizing she'd been holding her breath, she opened her lips and inhaled deeply. She went to the door and peered out the peep hole. An older couple strolled across the lot, their dog on a black leash sniffing the pavement.

Dina's mouth had gone as dry as old bones and her hands trembled.

"This is stupid." She grabbed up her backpack, locked the door behind her, and went out into the night, heading for the nearest bus station on the north bound side of the road. She didn't know where she was going, really, but she knew she needed a diversion if she were to remain calm. She must decide what she was going to do; stay in Ocean City, or move on to some other town.

She rode the city bus as far as it would take her, getting off at the 144th Street Transit Station. Instead of heading out toward Coastal Highway, instinct had her walking a block west, away from traffic, and then she cut south. She skirted behind the movie theater Gav had taken her to just days ago, cut through a neighborhood of single-wide trailers, and soon she saw the glow of holiday lights.

The closer she got to the lights, the more people she saw. She realized she'd come to Northside Park. The sign read Winterfest of Lights, and she remembered young Charlie telling her about the light display.

A line of people waited to take the tram ride to see the elaborate light exhibit, some of which were animated. Dina roamed through the Winterfest Village pavilion where she saw lots of parents with kids waiting for their turn to visit Santa while others sipped hot chocolate as they shopped for trinkets in the gift shop, all while jolly holiday tunes floated in the air. Dina could easily imagine how children could become swept away by the magic of the season.

Back outside, she paused at the edge of the crowd near the fence enclosure. She gazed out at the fancy lights—the drummer boy tapping his snare drum, a tall Christmas tree dazzling with thousands of crimson lights, golden-hued reindeer frozen mid-gallop, a huge American flag ablaze in patriotic red, white, and blue—and she suddenly realized how much she missed Gav. She'd have loved to share this with him. She'd spent time with him every day, and now his absence left her feeling lonely, bereft.

Of course, this desolation gnawing at her insides had a great deal to do with her fear of being discovered. Maybe she should just break down and tell Gav the whole sordid tale. At least then she wouldn't feel so all alone.

Her cell phone chirped. Hoping that Gav was calling to wish her a merry Christmas, she scrambled to dig the phone out of her coat pocket. Seeing *Mom* in the window, Dina tapped the screen.

"Hi, Mom," she greeted. "Merry Christmas."

"Merry Christmas, sweetheart."

Tension fringed her mother's voice and Dina frowned. "What's wrong? Did something happen? Are you and George okay?"

"We're fine," she said. "Really." Maria hesitated long enough to swallow. "I don't know that anything is wrong, really. It's just... well, George went out around lunch time to do some last minute shopping. You know how he loves to surprise me."

Dina did. Christmas morning was filled with gifts of tea light candles, glass baubles, little sweets, and angel figurines to add to her mother's menagerie.

"He just came home a bit ago." Apology coated her mom's voice when she added, "And he was reeking."

Pressing her lips together, Dina stifled the groan filling the back of her throat.

"Is he okay?"

"He is now," she said. "But he was pretty upset. Near to tears, actually, and he wanted me to call you. It seems that some young men came into the pub and offered to buy him a drink. It seems they were in the holiday spirit, and George said he didn't see the harm in celebrating with them.

"Especially if they were paying," Dina muttered.

"George said he'd never seen them in the pub before today," Maria said. "But they seemed to know you. After several rounds, they wanted to know where you were so they could wish you a merry Christmas."

Dina's heart pounded. Could the guys have been from the restaurant? She didn't think so. Harbor Bistro wasn't in the same area of town as the pub George frequented.

Her voice was a bit shaky when she asked, "Did he tell them anything?" Then she followed with, "Did *you* tell George where I am?"

"He's been worried, sweetheart. We both have."

"Mom!"

"I know. *I know.*"

Maria's worried voice became muffled as, Dina figured, she spoke to George.

"Mom, what did he tell them?"

"He can't remember," she told Dina. "His memory of the afternoon is hazy. He's not sure he said anything. Then again, he could have told them everything." Maria spoke louder. "It could be nothing. They could have been friends of yours from school. Or work. But George wanted me to call you."

"Because he knows it's not nothing." Anger flared, singeing her words.

"Honey, he didn't mean any harm. You know George loves you. I love you, too."

"Mom, I'm running. *Hiding*." Fury and fear lodged in her throat. "When someone is running, that means someone else is chasing. Or could be chasing."

"Sweetheart, maybe we should call the police—"

"You will not call the police!" Dina realized several people in the park looked askance at her. She took a deep, trembling breath. "Mom, you said all this happened at the pub this afternoon? Why are you just calling me now?"

"You know how he gets when he's drinking. He passed out at the pub. I told you, he just got home."

"I have to go. I have to find another place to stay." Ocean City was a pretty big town, but Dina still felt as frantic as a wild animal that had been cornered.

"Wait, Dina." She went silent for a moment. "Don't go in there."

"Don't go in where, Mom?"

"I don't know. But you will. I'm sure."

A shiver coursed across Dina's skin. Her

mother's warning took her aback. Then again, wasn't she always caught off guard by her mom's strange premonitions? The *weird words of wisdom*, as Dina had come to think of them, weren't even full-fledged predictions. They were merely thin slices of numinous foreboding that never seemed specific enough to be helpful at the time the words were uttered. Yet, the warnings were always helpful at some stage; the important point was to remain aware and remember at the right time.

Once when Dina had been in elementary school, her mother had told her at breakfast, "Just leave that be." Dina nor her mother hadn't a clue what the warning had been about, but that afternoon a teacher had dropped a glass bowl that had shattered on the floor. Before Dina could repeat her mother's warning, a little boy had gotten himself cut on the shards.

Then there had been the time her mother had called after the high school bell had signaled the end of the day. Dina had been on her way to the bus. "Don't get in that car," Maria had told her. Without thinking about it, Dina had reminded her, "I'm riding the bus, Mom." But the instant she'd hung up the phone and left the building, she'd run into a crowd of kids that had gathered to watch an argument that had broken out between two female classmates, notorious rivals who couldn't stand each other. The throng of students had been thick, and Dina had ended up missing the bus, as had several other kids. A guy from the senior class offered them a ride home, and while the others accepted, Dina had heeded her mother's advice. George had come to pick her up. The next day, Dina learned that the senior had run a red light and had been t-boned by an oncoming car. Thankfully, no one had been seriously hurt.

"Thanks, mom," Dina murmured. "I'll be careful. I really need to go now."

"But wait. How will I know where—"

"I'll call you. I promise." Dina ended the conversation, tucked her phone in her coat pocket, and headed out to Coastal Highway and the nearest bus stop.

The well-lit bus was empty save for her. And although the bus made stops all along the southward route, no one else boarded.

When she got off at her stop, the driver wished her happy holidays, and Dina offered him a tight-lipped smile. It was the best she could muster.

She ducked into the shadows as much as she could during the half-block walk to her hotel, and then hurried across the parking lot, her key in her hand. When she reached her room, she stopped and went completely still. Something looked off.

The wood near the knob looked mashed and there was a slight gap between the door and the jamb that she didn't remember having been there before. The window was dark and all was quiet. Did she chance going inside for her things?

A voice deep inside her shouted *no*. Then her mother's warning echoed in her head.

She looked out over the parking lot, her eyes darting from one shadow to another.

When had nighttime become so damned scary?

Go *some*where. Do *something*. *And do it now!*

She remembered she had Cathy's keys in her backpack. She hadn't told her mom she'd taken a job. George couldn't tell someone something he didn't know. She would be safe at the Sunshine Café. At first light, she'd find a way to get out of Ocean City.

Dina ran.

CHAPTER TEN

Dina floated in that odd, hazy state between sleep and wakefulness, a place where muscles turned to marshmallow and fear retreated to the fuzzy, outer edges of the mind. The high-pitched creaking of door hinges seeped into her lull and sent a shot of adrenalin through her. Her eyes popped open wide to see nothing but darkness.

For a split second, confusion reigned as she scrambled to remember where she was. She shifted in the tight confines, her muscles screaming, and the clatter of metal against the floor made her inhale sharply.

"Who's there?"

The unfamiliar male voice that called out shoved Dina's heart up into her throat. Then the ceiling light chased away the darkness and she squinted against the sudden brightness. She leaned forward just enough to deftly scoop up the weapon that had fallen from her limp fingers just seconds before, and then she did her best to squeeze back into the small, safe hiding place she'd found.

The man standing by the kitchen's back entryway sported an expensive looking black suit. His longish blond hair framed a handsome, tanned face, and he scanned the kitchen with piercingly blue eyes. He certainly didn't look like a drug dealer. Didn't look like he'd hang out with them, either. Even so, fear kept her frozen.

He hadn't seen Dina yet, and she held her breath in the hopes that he wouldn't.

The door hinges squealed again.

"Who are you talking to?" Cathy asked as she pushed her way into the café. "Everyone's waiting for ice up there."

The Christmas Eve party at the B&B upstairs. Dina had forgotten all about it.

"I heard something," the man told her.

"Oooo." Cathy shimmied up close to him. "Are you trying to scare me?"

The intimate teasing in Cathy's voice had Dina feeling self-conscious.

The guy reached up and placed quelling hands on Cathy's shoulders.

"I'm serious," he said. "Either someone is in here, or you've got a rat problem."

"Rats?" Cathy's gaze swung out toward the still-dark dining area, and then it lowered—zeroing in on Dina where she crouched under the counter.

"Dina?" Cathy frowned, stepping away from the man. "What are you doing there? Are you okay? What have you got...?" The lines between her eyes bit deeper. "Come out of there."

Her muscles stiff, Dina took several seconds to get out from under the counter and onto her feet, dragging her backpack with her.

"I was only going to stay until sunrise," Dina said. "What time is it, anyway?"

"It's a little after one," the man answered.

"Why are you hiding under there?" Cathy took a step closer, her pretty black cocktail dress rustling against her thighs. "Maybe what I should be asking is... who are hiding from?"

"Would you mind turning off the light?" Dina glanced over her shoulder toward the big picture window looking out onto the boardwalk in front of the café. "I mean, we're safe and all. No one knows I'm here, but I'd feel better if—"

"If that's true," Cathy cut her off. "If you're safe, why are clutching my meat cleaver like you're ready to chop off someone's fingers?"

The guy touched Cathy's arm. "Should I call the police?"

"No!" Dina's tone was sharp as a bursting balloon, and she murmured a quick apology before directing her eyes toward the floor. Then she looked up at Cathy. "I'll leave now. It's okay. I'll be fine."

Cathy crossed her arms. "You're not going anywhere until we talk." She tipped her head. "Let's go into my office. We'll shut the door. No one will see us in there." She turned her attention to the man at her side. "Brad, would you grab some ice and take it upstairs? Don't say anything to them about Dina just yet, okay?"

He looked from Cathy to Dina and back again, clearly undecided about leaving Cathy alone with a deranged, cleaver-wielding woman.

"Nothing's going to happen," Cathy said, seeming to read his mind. "I don't know what's going on." She walked up to Dina and gently plucked the cleaver from her hand. "But I'm going to find out, that's for damned sure."

"Okay, okay," he relented. "But I'm coming right back down here."

Cathy's office was only big enough for a desk, a chair, a tall, narrow file cabinet, and a small loveseat. It was familiar to Dina because it also acted as the break room, a place where Dina could get off her feet in private for a few minutes when there was a lull between customers.

"Sit down, Dina."

Cathy rounded her desk and settled in the chair.

"So what's going on?"

Dina chewed her upper lip, hugging her backpack to her chest. Finally, she said, "You don't want to get mixed up in this. If you'll just let me stay here until morning, I'll catch the next Greyhound out of town."

She could tell from the set of Cathy's jaw that she wouldn't be going anywhere without an argument.

"Honey," Cathy said, her tone soft, "if you're running from the police, you need to tell me."

Dina shook her head. "Cathy, please, just let me go." She stood up and slung the strap of her backpack over one shoulder. "I don't have to wait until morning."

Cathy stood up, too. "You're obviously in trouble, Dina. Something has scared the devil out of you. Why won't you let me help you?"

"Because it's not fair of me to drag you into this mess I've gotten myself caught up in." Unexpected tears sprang to her eyes. "You've been wonderful to me. You gave me a job. Fed me twice a day. And you let me keep working even when I refused to tell you my full name and address. You *helped* me. You didn't have to do any of that. I am not going to repay your kindness with—"

Emotion clogged her throat and strangled off the rest of her sentence.

"Dina." Cathy came back around the desk, lifting her hands and placing them on Dina's upper arms. "If you won't tell me what's going on, at least let me call for help. I'll call someone you trust. "

The tears welling in her eyes overflowed, streaming in fat, hot droplets down her cheeks.

Her voice sounded like rusty nails being pried from old wood when she said, "I don't trust the police."

Cathy studied her face intently for several seconds, and then she said, "Gav, then. Let's call Gav. He's your friend. He's become more than that. Anyone can see it. He'll help you, Dina. He's a good man. He would never betray you. You know that just as well as I do."

Thoughts and implications and what-ifs spun through Dina's mind like a wicked tornado, ripping and tearing at her emotions.

"He *is* a good man," she agreed on a sob. "I can't involve him. He's a cop. Once he finds out... once I tell him my story... I don't know what he'd be legally bound to do. He could lose his job. And he's not in town, anyway. He's spending Christmas Eve with his family. I can't intrude on—"

"He would *want* you to intrude, honey," Cathy insisted. "In fact, he'd be upset that you didn't. And it's not Christmas Eve any longer." She lifted her shoulders in a shrug. "It's Christmas Day. You told me he has to work. He has to come back to Ocean City today anyway."

Dina sniffed and shook her head in utter misery.

"That's a horrible argument for waking a man in the middle of the night."

Despite her worry, Cathy grinned. "Okay, so my reasoning on that one wasn't so good. But I'm feeling desperate." Her tone flattened with deep gravity as she added, "And so are you."

The bare-bones truth in Cathy's statement took all the fight out of Dina. Her shoulders sagged as she stared into Cathy's compassionate gaze, her lips pressing into a thin line.

Dina couldn't deny it; desperation had become like a second skin, stifling, smothering. She simply couldn't live with it any longer.

"You have his number programmed in your phone?" Cathy asked.

Dina gave a single, mute nod.

Cathy held out her hand. "Give it to me. I'll call him."

CHAPTER ELEVEN

———

"**I** thought you weren't coming home until Christmas morning, Gav."

An herby aroma wafted under Dina's nose when Gav set the steaming mug in front of her on the table. He slid into the chair adjacent from hers.

"I don't know what happened to make you come home early," she added. "But I'm so glad you're here."

When Cathy had hung up the phone from speaking with Gav, she'd told Dina that he'd already started home; that he'd been waiting at a traffic light in Selbyville, so it hadn't taken him long at all to reach them. Cathy hadn't left Dina alone for even a minute, and her friend Brad had returned to wait with them for Gav to arrive.

Having him near had an amazingly calming effect on Dina. She'd felt it the moment he'd walked through the back door at the café. The instinct to run to him, bury her face in his chest, had been strong, but she'd resisted. She'd known him such a short time, yet the depth of her faith in him staggered her. She knew in her heart he was solid and trustworthy.

The first few minutes had been flat-out awkward. Gav plowed in, wanting information, details she felt uncomfortable revealing in front of Cathy and her friend. Gav had grabbed up her backpack, he'd thanked Cathy for calling him, and he'd taken Dina's hand and hauled her to her feet. Now they sat at his kitchen table, the room lit only by the glow of the low-wattage fixture over the sink.

He lived in Little Salisbury, one of the older neighborhoods in town, he'd told her. His ranch house was small and the neatness of the rooms told her he liked things in their proper place.

His mug grazed against the wood tabletop when he slid it closer to him. "I couldn't sleep. I loved seeing mom and dad, and my brothers. But... I had this strange feeling. I couldn't shake it. I missed you." He lifted his shoulders. "I hated the thought that you were here all alone. I thought that, if I could get back here, maybe we could have breakfast together... or something. Before I had to go to work."

His mouth quirked up on one side, and the sexiness of it sparked a vague, whispery heat low in the pit of Dina's belly. She reached over and curled her fingers over the corded muscles of his forearm.

"I'm relieved you're here. Honestly."

"Cathy said you were terrified when she found you."

Now was the time. She had to tell him.

She pulled her hand away from him, laced her fingers around the warm mug. "I think he found my step-dad. I'm not sure. But—"

"Who?" Gav asked. "Who are we talking about?"

Dina exhaled fully before she revealed, "His name is Joseph Richardson. I think he, or people he knows, found George. In the pub earlier today. They bought him drinks. Lots of drinks, judging from what my mom said. And George might have told them where I am."

Gav nodded. "Okay, so who's this Joseph Richardson? How do you know him? Is he an old boyfriend or something? Is he harassing you? Stalking you? Abusing you?"

"I don't know him. I *saw* him. On a street corner." She paused, licked her lips. "He sells drugs. In Baltimore. I'm a witness. To a crime. And the judge postponed the court date until after the New Year. My attorney said this would be over before Christmas, but the judge put off the—"

"Wait. Just stop a second."

His hand was warm when he gently grasped her wrist.

"I want you to start at the beginning."

So she did. She told him how, back in the summer, the woman in charge of catering services at the restaurant where she worked had been scheduled for minor surgery, and how her boss had asked Dina to drive into Baltimore to meet with a catering client, and how she'd become hopelessly lost in the narrow streets of a rundown neighborhood.

"I was sitting at a red light," she told him.

"Trying to find an entrance ramp to I-95. I'm sure I took the wrong exit. I heard yelling, and I saw three men on the corner. One had a gun, shouting, waving it around. Then another of the guys pulled out a pistol and shot the guy who'd been out of control. But the first guy returned fire. The third man, the paper called him Joseph "Snag" Richardson; anyway, he stood there like some kind of marble statue. I don't know if it was fear or disbelief. I heard police sirens almost instantly."

She closed her eyes, the memory filling her with dread. "Richardson's eyes... I'll never forget. They were wild. Once he snapped out of that frozen state, he looked like some feral animal. He made eye-to-eye contact with me. For a minute, I thought he was going to bolt toward me. But then he ran off down an alleyway." She swallowed before whispering, "The other two men lay sprawled on the sidewalk. They died. Right there. I had never seen so much blood in my life."

Gav seemed to understand the drill she'd gone through after witnessing the shootings; giving the police her statement, ID'ing Richardson in a lineup, agreeing to testify, retaining an attorney.

Being in the wrong place at the wrong time had cost her a lot of time, money, and sleepless nights.

"What I don't understand is," Gav said, "why you felt you had to run. I mean, the police ask witnesses to testify all the time. It's the only sure way of putting criminals in prison. If you didn't feel safe, why didn't you go to the police?"

"That's just it. I didn't even know I was in danger until..."

Gav frowned when she let the rest of her sentence fade away.

"Until what?" he quietly pressed.

"Listen, what I'm about to say is going to sound crazy." She leaned back in her chair. "But I need for you to believe me."

He remained silent, but his grip on her wrist became snugger and he roved his thumb over her skin. She took it as a combination of his silent assurance and encouragement.

"The day the judge postponed the hearing," she began, "I got a call from a Detective Stewart. He told me they had reason to believe I was in danger. That they wanted to put me up at a hotel over Christmas. I didn't want to. It being the holiday and all. But Mom and George thought it was a good idea. The detective said I'd have a uniformed police guard with me until I testified."

"So when does the crazy part start?" he asked. "Everything you've said seems logical to me."

"The very first night in the hotel, the police officer said he was going out for sodas and pizza. He asked if I wanted anything. I have to tell you, at first I was shocked. And a little scared. If they thought I was in danger, why would the cop leave me alone?"

"You're right. That doesn't make sense."

"I started contemplating being in that tiny room for two weeks." Even now, the thought made her gulp in a lungful of air. "Made me claustrophobic. I went to the window, and that's when I saw them."

Gav let go of her wrist. "Them?"

"The officer. And Richardson. They were just down the block. And the cop took something from Richardson before walking on down the street."

"Took what?"

"I don't know. I didn't hang around long enough to find out. I grabbed my bag and I left."

"Are you certain it was Richardson?"

She nodded. "He has a jagged scar above his right eyebrow. It was him. I'm positive." Telling the story, reliving those moments, made her skin itch, made her feel like she needed to get up and move around. "I didn't know what to do, Gav. That cop had picked me up and driven me out in the middle of nowhere to that hotel. I didn't have a car. I grabbed my bag and left. I found an ATM, and then I headed for the Greyhound bus station. I was afraid to go home. Afraid that, once they found me gone, they'd go right to my apartment. So I hopped on a bus."

The space between Gav's eyebrows was notched with lines. "And you think Richardson is in town. Here. In OC."

"Well, if my picture in the papers and on the news didn't reveal my whereabouts," she said, "I'm afraid George must have."

The lines on his brow deepened. "And that's what terrified you? Finding out that your step-father might have talked to this guy?"

"No, it was seeing the door to my room tonight," she said. "I went up to Northside Park to kill some time. When I got back, my door looked like it had been tampered with. Pried open. Something."

Gav stood up. "Why the hell didn't you say that before, Dina? He could have been in there." He moved into the living room and grabbed his coat from where he'd tossed it on a chair when they'd come in.

She picked up her coat and slipped one arm into a sleeve.

"No," he told her. "You stay here. I'm calling for help. We'll check it out."

"I'm going with you."

"You're staying here. I mean it."

Once she'd shrugged her way into her coat, she zipped it up in one quick motion. "I'm going. If you find him, you'll need me to tell you if you have the right guy."

* * *

The trip to her hotel near downtown took them mere minutes. The drive took on a peculiar note; seeing the bright, festive lights decorating the street lamps, trees in the median strips, the businesses, and homes put an odd twist on the anxiety lying heavy in her gut. This time of year should be happy and light and exciting. She didn't feel any of those things.

Gav called the station during the drive. The entire building looked dark when they arrived.

Dina inhaled a soft, sharp breath when she noticed the police cars tucked back in the shadows on the side street.

"Four cruisers? What if the room is empty? What if I'm wasting everyone's—"

"Dispatch wouldn't have sent them if they hadn't been free." Gav put his car in park but left the engine running. He turned and looked at her sternly. "Stay here. Don't move. I don't want any argument, Dina."

"I'm not arguing."

"Give me your room key," he said. "Just in case I need it."

She placed it in his palm without saying another word. As they had driven south on Coastal Highway, Dina had felt a tension building in Gav. He'd grown pensive, and she realized he must be readying himself for facing what might turn into a dangerous situation. He was focused, attentive, centered. This professional side of him made her feel... *safe*... and very much cared for. His willingness to put himself in jeopardy in order to help her stirred a deep gratitude in her. And something else. Something she couldn't put a name to.

This was something he did every day on the job. Her admiration for him swelled to the bursting point.

He exited the car, closing his door as softly as possible, and Dina watched as the other cops stepped out onto the street. They talked in low voices for mere seconds and then they headed toward her hotel room.

Nerves skittered in her chest like droplets of water on a hot skillet. Pressing the button to lower the window a few inches, she relished the cool breeze that seeped inside the car. The urge to turn off the heater was strong, but she couldn't take her eyes off Gav's broad back as he approached the door.

He disappeared inside as did at least five other officers.

Quiet hovered in the night air. She heard some shouting, tussling, and thumping. And then it was over.

Light spilled out into the parking lot from the open doorway and she heard more raised voices. The need to get on her feet, to get out into the wide open space, overwhelmed her, and it took every ounce of her self-control to remain in the car as Gav had instructed.

Several long minutes later, the officers filed out of the motel room, and Gav led a hand-cuffed Joseph Richardson toward the police cars. The last cop out of the room carried what looked like a large stick, and when he got closer, Dina saw it was a metal baseball bat. Icy claws raked the length of her spine.

Richardson's gaze happened upon her. His jaw set and he glared, then he shouted, "You bitch!"

The man continued to spew hate and anger, even after Gav growled out a warning and planted his palm on the crown of Richardson's head, guiding him into the backseat of one of the police cars.

The group of cops continued to talk, and a few minutes later they began to go their separate ways. When the last cruiser had pulled away from the curb, Dina opened the car door and stepped out onto the sidewalk. She slowly sucked in the fresh air, hoping it would calm the queasiness in her stomach.

Gav came toward her. "We'll have to go inside and gather up your things."

"Maybe I should—"

"You're coming home with me."

His sharp retort sliced through her thought so cleanly, she couldn't even remember what she'd meant to say.

"The lock on the door is broken," he said. "And besides that..." He came closer and wrapped his arms around her. "I need a little time. I'm not trying to tell you what to do. It's just that I need to know you're safe. And you will be. With me."

The tone of his voice was gruff and in direct opposition to the gentleness of his embrace. Dina instinctively knew he was still upset about what he'd just gone through—finding a criminal waiting for her in her room, grappling with the weight of what could have happened to her.

She reached her arms around his waist, sliding her hands across his back, and she knew she was taking as much comfort as she gave. More, probably.

He kissed the top of her head and groaned. "Why didn't you trust me with this, Dina? I could have been watching closer. You should have told me."

She whispered against his chest, "I was afraid

you'd call the Baltimore police. Because of that badge of yours, I thought you'd have no other choice but to let them know I was here."

The warm scent of him wafted around her and she sighed. Then he pulled back just enough so that he could tip up her chin and force her to look him in the eyes.

"You must have been scared to death this whole time," he said.

Her mouth curled slightly. "I'd be lying if I said I wasn't afraid," she admitted. "But not the whole time. Whenever I was with you..."

The look in his dark eyes intensified as he studied her, his gaze touching her hair, her forehead, her nose, her chin.

And then he kissed her lightly, once, twice, three times. His lips lingered on hers with slowly mounting pressure. He deepened the kiss into a bold and hungry attack, and Dina realized she was ravenous for the taste of him.

Her breathing came in labored draws when they parted, the December air cool against her hot, damp mouth. Her heart pounded and need pulsed like a base drum between her thighs... and here she was, standing outside on the sidewalk in the wee hours of the morning.

"Seems I am *always* in the wrong place at the wrong time." She grinned up at him.

"Ain't that the truth?"

A chuckle bubbled up from deep in her throat. "Did you kiss me like that because I'm a damsel in distress?"

"You know exactly why I kissed you like that," he told her. "I think I've been clear about how I feel about you. You're the one who's been ducking and dodging the issue."

"Hey!" She gave him a little nudge with her shoulder. "I've been a little preoccupied, you know." His conceding nod warmed her heart. "I didn't think it was a good idea to... you know, start anything, or get involved. Not while all this awful crap was hanging over my head."

He sighed. "Well, the crap is officially headed to jail. And I'll see to it that he won't be offered bail. With these charges in OC added to the charges he's facing in Baltimore, I think he'll be tied up for a good, long time. So there's nothing to fear. Absolutely nothing."

She rested her forehead on his chest, breathed in

the heat of him, enjoyed the happy buoyancy that filled her like a rising tide.

"Of course," he murmured quietly, "we still have to deal with Detective Stewart. And the officer who took you to that hotel. Do you remember his name?"

"Price," she told him. "That was the name on his badge. I don't know his first name."

"That's okay. We'll find him. And if they aren't able to offer up a good explanation, there's going to be hell to pay."

Dina looked up into his face. "You know, not every damsel gets her very own knight in shining armor."

"You're no damsel," he groused. "You're a stubborn, stubborn woman who should have confided in me. I could have protected you. I could have—"

"Hey. Stop. I'm okay," she assured him.

He hugged her then, tightly. "I am so damned glad nothing happened to you, Dina."

"Me, too," she whispered. "And now that you know all my secrets, I'd like to... you know..." She arched her brows. "Let's go back to your house. I want you to unwrap me like a Christmas present."

Her gaze meandered over his face, and she let her expression convey every nuance of her desire for him.

Gav groaned. "Honey, I'd love nothing better, believe me. But once I get you settled, I have to head back to the station. I've got enough paperwork in front of me to fill Santa's velvet sack."

Then his mouth went flat. "Now that we got this guy," he said, "are you going home? Your mom is probably—"

"Are you kidding me?" she said. "I'm spending Christmas with you. And New Year's, too. If you'll let me."

The expression on his handsome face eased, and then he kissed her on the tip of the nose.

"I cannot wait to unwrap my Christmas present," he said.

She reached up and slid her fingers behind his neck. "I can't wait to be unwrapped."

Anticipation glittered in his sexy brown eyes and his mouth came down to claim hers.

CHAPTER TWELVE

Steel-colored clouds blanketed the sky on the January day Dina testified against Joseph Richardson. The man's brazen attempt to silence a witness to his crime had resulted in a story about him in the Baltimore Sun. "Snag," as he was known on the street, had grown up without a father. His birth mother, a prostitute who had been in and out of mental health facilities during Richardson's childhood, hadn't been able to care for herself, let alone her son. Poverty-stricken and alone, Richardson had become a petty thief early on in his life. He'd acquired his nickname during his very first run-in with the law when, in attempting to escape police, he'd climbed a fence topped with barbed wire and ended up with seventeen stitches just above his eye. Richardson's crimes had steadily escalated until that fateful day he'd been approached by two desperate addicts when he'd only had one bag left to sell. The ensuing argument between the junkies had soared like a heat-seeking missile, resulting in two deaths that day.

The Sun reporter attempted to paint Richardson as a victim of a deplorable upbringing, but Dina refused to buy into that. Plenty of people grew up poor who didn't end up providing for themselves by preying on others.

Just as Gav had suggested, she had kept her eyes directed on the lawyer who had questioned her and avoided looking at Richardson. After stepping out of the witness box, she'd felt fifty pounds lighter.

She sloshed through the gray watery snow on the courthouse steps and paused long enough to scan the crowd. Her gaze met Gav's, and suddenly the dreary day felt more like mid-summer. They immediately moved toward each other. On the bottom step, he slid his arms around her.

"You were perfect," he said. "Clear, concise, and you didn't hesitate or stammer on a single question. A prosecutor's dream."

The defending attorney hadn't pressed her too badly. All in all, telling her story hadn't been nearly as difficult as she'd imagined.

"I was nervous," she told Gav. "And I'm glad it's over, but I'm also happy I did it." She reached up on her tip-toes and kissed Gav on the cheek. "When I wasn't focused on the lawyers and the judge, I looked at you. That made it easier. Thanks for being here."

He just smiled and hugged her. They had done a lot of that, lately. Hugging. Holding hands. It seemed every time their eyes met, they shared a smile.

The past two weeks had been a blissful dream. Yes, Gav had worked on Christmas Day, but she'd spent the hours waiting for him baking a pie and cooking a nice dinner. They'd both been so exhausted from staying up the night before that they'd fallen asleep soon after they had eaten. Needless to say, the intimate "unwrapping" that they'd so looked forward to had been postponed.

However, waking up next to him, cradled in his arms, had been nothing short of heaven on earth.

After having caught up on their sleep, they'd spent the remaining nights getting to know one another... exploring each other's bodies in delectable ways.

When she wasn't working at the café and he wasn't on duty, they had talked and laughed, and talked some more. Several things became abundantly clear to Dina; she genuinely liked this man, she enjoyed being with him, and when they were apart, she thought a lot about him. He had this way of looking at her that let her know he wanted her, not just physically, although that was wonderful, but he wasn't afraid to show her that she captivated him, enchanted him, fascinated him. With one look he could instill an amazing self-confidence in her. No one had ever made her feel the way Gav made her feel.

As if he were reading her thoughts, he whispered against her ear, "I wish I could explain how you make me feel."

"Happy?" she supplied.

"Yeah. Very. But it's even more than that." He kissed her temple and then gazed into her face.

"You make me feel light and breezy and... and... energetic." He grinned. "In the cheesiest way imaginable."

When their laughter subsided, his gaze turned serious. "I realize we've known each other for less than a month, but it seems much longer to me."

"Me, too," she agreed.

"Dina, I don't want to scare you," he said. "But I think I could be falling in love with you."

Her gaze widened, and when she opened her mouth to speak, he touched her lips with his index finger.

"You don't have to say anything," he murmured. "We have plenty of time to get to know each other."

She reached up, took his hand between both of hers, and softly kissed the warm pad of his finger. "You couldn't scare me if you tried. But... before you start deciding how you feel about me, you need to meet my parents. You already know about George's problem, but you haven't met my mother yet."

His mouth screwed up, playfully. "How bad can she be?"

"Oh, she's not bad," Dina said. "She's very good.

In fact, I'm sure you'll find out she's very... accurate."

"What is she? A sharp shooter?"

"You could call her that, yes." Dina chuckled. "Sans the bullets, of course."

"I have no idea what you're talking about. And I don't care what your mom does, or how she does it." Gav pulled her tight against him and a powerful fervency pervaded the small space between them. "As long as I'm with you, nothing else matters."

It was crazy how quickly this man has stolen her heart, and she his, it seemed.

"You need to meet my parents, Gav," she stressed. She wanted nothing more than to assure him she felt the same as he, but her mother's premonitions might be too weird for him to handle. If that turned out to be the case, he would need an out, and she intended to graciously allow him that much.

He inched closer, clearly intent on kissing away her doubts.

"Dina? Sweetheart?"

Her mother's voice brought the intimate moment to a screeching halt, and Dina and Gav stepped away from each other.

"I thought we'd never find you. This place is worse than a zoo."

"Mom." Dina descended the final courthouse step and gave her mother a quick hug. "Thanks for coming."

"We wanted to be here for you. We know how hard this has been for you."

She hugged her step-father. "Hi, George. It's good to see you both."

"Dina, I want to tell you how sorry I am." George's facial features sagged. "I don't even remember what I told those men. It's just shameful."

"It's okay, George," she assured him yet again. "I'm okay."

He'd apologized at least half a dozen times on the phone since the Christmas Eve incident. He took his step-daughter's hand in his.

"But I put you in danger." Sadness made his silvery blue eyes water. "I want you to know I will never drink another drop again. Never."

A small, consoling smile tugged at Dina's mouth, and she wrapped her arms around him. She knew this man to be kind and gentle, someone who wouldn't ever knowingly hurt a living soul. But she also knew him to be weak. She and her mother had both heard that same promise many times over the years, and up to this point in their lives, it had been a promise he'd been incapable of keeping. Dina was content to take him at his word, yet again. She knew in her heart that, at this moment, he intended to hold to his conviction. And who knew? Maybe he could hold that monster called The Taste at bay this time.

"Mom, George," Dina said. "I want you to meet someone."

She swung her arm wide, and Gav joined her on the sidewalk.

Her mother's green eyes sparkled. "Is this the police officer you told us about?"

"It is."

"I've had some good feelings about him." The woman nodded.

Dina grinned. "So have I."

When Dina looked at Gav, she couldn't help but smile. Her heart raced and she felt the need to take a deep, calming breath. "This is Officer Gav Thomas," she told her parents. She tucked her hand through the crook of Gav's arm. "Gav, this is Maria and George Dillon. My mom and step-dad."

"Gavreel." Delight put a twinkle in Maria's tone. "It's so nice to meet you."

Gav darted a glance at Dina, a silent question in stunned expression. She shook her head to let him know she hadn't told her mother about his namesake.

"We'll talk later," Dina promised Gav.

Before Dina could say more, her mom had enveloped Gav in a jovial hug. "Thank the angels among us! I prayed and prayed for Dina's protection." Maria pulled back, but hung on to the sleeves of his coat as if she thought he might fly away. "I prayed for them to send her someone who could bring her peace." She offered Gav and Dina the broadest of smiles. "You, Gavreel, were the answer to my prayers."

A delightful energy swirled around them all, and Maria hugged Gav a second time. "Your mother must be a *very* spiritual lady."

Once he'd extricated himself from Maria's embrace, he nodded and told her, "She's an extremely devout Catholic."

Without pause, Maria replied, "I won't hold that against her."

Dina gasped. "*Mother!*"

"I'm teasing, Dina."

George nodded. "She's teasing."

Dina's step-dad leaned forward to shake hands with Gav.

Maria said, "Now that this nasty business is over, let's go have lunch. I'm starved." She paused, as if struck by an insistent thought. "Dina, honey, you need to say yes."

"Of course, I'll say yes to lunch."

"Not lunch. It's something else. Something important. Something personal. I'm not sure exactly." Maria blinked, and her lips spread to reveal her teeth. "But you will, I'm sure of it." Then her gaze cut to Gav. "And you need to know there really *are* no bullets." Her laugh was like the ringing of tiny bells. "Now that's downright silly. You're a police officer. Of course, there are bullets. I don't make this stuff up. I just say it like I hear it."

Maria shrugged and turned to her husband. "Now, George, let's go find a place to eat."

Dina watched her parents walk away from them, and she slowly swiveled her head to cast a sidelong glance at Gav. As she feared, an obvious uneasiness shadowed his dark eyes and marred his brow as he stared after Maria.

Then he looked at Dina. "Wow," he whispered. Air whooshed from him in a sigh and he shook his head. But he took only seconds to recover.

He captured her chin in his fingers. "There are no bullets." Humor twisted his mouth. "I get that. So, Dina, listen to your mother. Say yes."

"But..." She hesitated, then finished, "weren't you freaked out by my mom?"

"Hell, yeah, I'm freaked out. But at the same time, it's kinda cool, you know?"

She only nodded.

He bumped her shoulder with his. "I'm a little insulted that you'd think I couldn't handle it. I'm no sissy."

"This is true." She immediately thought back to Christmas Eve, and how he'd stormed into her hotel room with such fearlessness. "You're no sissy. Not even close."

The compliment pleased him.

He bumped her shoulder again, his eyes glittering. "So say it. Say yes, Dina. To us."

Happiness scampered across her skin, raising the tiny hairs on her arms and sending her blood thrumming through her body.

"Okay, Gav," she breathed. "I say yes."

He kissed her, quick and hard. Then they laced their fingers and hurried down the slushy sidewalk in search of lunch.

A Note From the Author

Dear Reader,

Thank you for taking the time to read GROWN UP CHRISTMAS LIST. If you enjoyed the story, please consider leaving a review or telling a friend about the book. There is no better advertisement than word-of-mouth from someone who liked the story. As an independent author, I really could use your help! Thanks so much.

Sometimes a book's characters surprise me. I don't usually write stories with an element of suspense, but when Dina began talking to me, I quickly understood that's where she was taking me. I wasn't all that surprised when Dina's mother showed up with her quirky ability to "know" things. I am fascinated by the idea of paranormal talent. I feel the addition added a little fun to the story. I hope you do, too.

There are other stories in the Ocean City Boardwalk series:

FOLLOWING HIS HEART, Book 1

TWO HEARTS IN WINTER, Book 2

WILD HEARTS OF SUMMER, Book 3

AN ALMOST PERFECT CHRISTMAS, Book 4

THE WEDDING PLANNER'S SON, Book 6

I hope you'll look for them!

My very best,
Donna Fasano

FOLLOWING HIS HEART, Ocean City Boardwalk Series, Book 1

Sara Carson is a 30-something widow with a busy life. Two fun-loving best friends, a caring mom who needs her, and a thriving sweet shop. What more could a woman want? But when the ancient plumbing in her shop springs a leak and a gorgeous, dark-eyed stranger rushes to her rescue, hilarity unfolds—and Sara quickly sees exactly what she's been missing.

Something most peculiar draws Landon Richards to Ocean City, Maryland—and to the lovely Sara. This woman touches his heart like no other, and the two of them explore the heady attraction that pulses between them. But haunting dreams have a way of encroaching on reality, and the strange phenomenon that brings these two together will also threaten to tear them apart.

Available in paperback and for Kindle, Nook, iBooks, Kobo, and Google Play.

TWO HEARTS IN WINTER, Ocean City Boardwalk Series, Book 2

Loss and betrayal have caused Heather Phillips to give up on love. She's thrown herself into running The Lonely Loon, her Bed and Breakfast located on the boardwalk of Ocean City, Maryland. The "off season" in this tourist town is usually a time of rest and reflection for her; however, DB Atwell, a famous author, arrives at The Loon for the winter to finish his long-overdue novel. Daniel, too, has faced grief, and tragedy continues to haunt him. Once Heather and Daniel meet, their lives will never be the same.

Reminiscent of Nights in Rodanthe by Nicholas Sparks and culminating in a happily-ever-after similar to the great Nora Roberts, Two Hearts in Winter is a story about learning to let go of the past, about realizing that, though hardship affects us, it need not define us, and about coming to understand and truly believe that beauty is sometimes covered in scars. The human heart has an amazing ability to forgive, to heal, and to hope, especially when touched by love.

Available in paperback and for Kindle, Nook, iBooks, Kobo, and Google Play.

WILD HEARTS OF SUMMER, Ocean City Boardwalk Series, Book 3

Cathy Whitley's two best friends, Sara and Heather, may have found the men of their dreams... and that's all well and good for them. But that's not going to happen to Cathy. She allowed love to catch her off-guard once and it drained her dry, emotionally and financially. She'll never let it happen again. Ever.

Brad Henderson has been chasing Cathy for years. He's settled for their on-again-off-again, "friends with bennies" relationship for far longer than he expected. Attempting to scale the stone wall she's built around her heart has left him scraped and bruised. When he inherits a business worth millions, he is sure she'll see him in a new light. Right?

One way or the other, it's time to draw a line in the sand...

Available February 2017 in paperback and for Kindle, Nook, iBooks, Kobo, and Google Play.

AN ALMOST PERFECT CHRISTMAS, Ocean City Boardwalk Series, Book 4

When it comes to business, Aaron Chase knows how to succeed. But when his daughter, Izzie, asks him for the perfect family Christmas, the handsome widower feels at a loss about how to make his little girl's dream come true.

Pediatric Nurse Christy Cooper has dedicated her life to taking care of children. She agrees to act as Izzie's stand-in mom for this special holiday and throws herself into making the child's Christmas wish a reality. Maybe this selfless act will somehow alleviate her secret regrets and failures of the past.

The holiday is filled with fun and laughter, and it's amazing how three short days can be so life-changing. When the impish eight-year-old talks the adults into acting out a silly, make-believe wedding, young Izzie is certain the magic of the season will turn the pretend vows into the real thing. The little girl wants her daddy to have Christmas in his life—every single day.

Available in paperback and for Kindle, Nook, iBooks, Kobo, and Google Play.

GROWN UP CHRISTMAS LIST, Ocean City Boardwalk Series, Book 5

Dina Griffin flees a dangerous situation and ends up in Ocean City, Maryland where she hopes to spend the holidays in hiding. Trusting no one, she wants only one thing this Christmas—to feel safe. Then Officer Gav Thomas threatens to arrest her for shoplifting. *Shoplifting?*

Gav is certain there's something Dina isn't telling him about her visit to his seaside town, so he devises a means to stick close to the vulnerable beauty. An unexpected attraction sparks, fierce enough to heat up the salt-tinged, wintry nights.

But the trouble Dina had hoped to escape arrives at her doorstep, bringing with it stark-raving fear and the realization that she *must* place her trust in someone.

Is Gav really just a local cop... or is he Dina's guardian angel?

Available now in paperback and for Kindle, Nook, iBooks, Kobo, and Google Play.

THE WEDDING PLANNER'S SON, Ocean City Boardwalk Series, Book 6

Tawny is a driven, high-achiever who fully expects to someday run the family business. But when her corporate exec parents attempt to use her as a pawn, Tawny flees to the only place she's ever felt happy—the beach.

Jack Barclay spends his summer days creating romantic seaside weddings for lovers. His laid-back attitude has served him well over the years. Stressing out about work only causes a person to miss the best parts of life.

Jack and Tawny are as different as sea and sky,

but the fascination they find in each others company can't be denied. So they embark on a temporary, no-strings-attached romance with eyes wide open. What could possibly go wrong?

Coming, Spring 2017, in paperback and for Kindle, Nook, iBooks, Kobo, and Google Play.

About The Author

Donna Fasano is a USA TODAY Bestselling Author whose books have sold nearly 4 million copies worldwide and have been translated into two dozen languages. She lives on Maryland's Eastern Shore with her husband and Roo, their twelve-year-old Australian cattle dog mix.

Other Books by Donna Fasano

Following His Heart, Ocean City Boardwalk Series,
Book 1
Two Hearts In Winter, Ocean City Boardwalk
Series, Book 2
Wild Hearts of Summer, Ocean City Boardwalk
Series, Book 3
An Almost Perfect Christmas, Ocean City
Boardwalk Series, Book 4
Grown-Up Christmas List, Ocean City Boardwalk
Series, Book 5
The Wedding Planner's Son, Ocean City
Boardwalk Series, Book 6
Reclaim My Heart
The Merry-Go-Round
Her Fake Romance
The Single Daddy Club Series: Derrick, Book 1

The Single Daddy Club Series: Jason, Book 2
The Single Daddy Club Series: Reece, Book 3
Take Me, I'm Yours
His Wife for a While
An Accidental Family
Mountain Laurel
A Beautiful Stranger, A Family Forever, Book 1
and others

Non-fiction Books
Prayer of Quiet
Favorite Christmas Cookies
Recipes of Love
Guy Food

Made in United States
Orlando, FL
02 December 2022

25395576R10100